WHERE I
NEED TO BE

BY

KIMBERLY KNIGHT

DEDICATION

*For my family, friends, my Smutty Mafia ladies,
and to all who have supported me
through this crazy journey.*

TABLE OF CONTENTS

CHAPTER ONE

When life hands you lemons, they say to make lemonade. Well, life just handed me a whole lemon tree. Three weeks ago, I felt like nothing in my life could go wrong. I was in Hawaii with my best friend, Ryan Kennedy, her boyfriend, Max, and who I had thought to be the love of my life, Travis.

Travis and I met almost two years before at a New Year's Eve party that Ryan invited me to. Her boyfriend had just made partner at his law firm and threw a huge party at his house to celebrate his promotion and ring in the New Year.

Travis was an attorney at the firm as well and I would like to say it was love at first sight, but looking back, it was never love. I was instantly attracted to Travis but it had taken us a few dates to actually click. He had short brown hair, green eyes and a sweet, innocent, charming side to him. The side that opened doors for you, pulled out your chair and even cooked and cleaned up after himself. I thought I had met the one. *Wrong.*

"Alright, Spencer Marshall, it is time to get your *ass* off the couch and start acting like you have a life again," Ryan said as she came storming into our house stomping on the hardwood floors with her heels. She stopped walking when she reached the couch I was sitting on––the couch which was starting to grow accustomed to my daily and nightly ritual and had formed the perfect indention of my butt. "You have been moping around here for two weeks and I am no longer going to let my best friend waste her life away over a guy."

"Go away!" I shouted at her as I stuffed my face with a spoonful of mint chocolate chip ice cream. "I'm fine." Ryan was right though, I needed to stop moping. My mom always told me that no man was worth my tears. But in all honesty, after dating someone for almost two years, aren't you allowed a few tears and some depression after you walk into his office and find him banging his secretary on his desk? I had just wanted to surprise him and take him to lunch. Didn't realize he had a surprise for me, too.

"Tomorrow night I'm going to scope out that new gym Club 24 that opened near my office. My boss is writing a story about it and asked me to use the free two-week membership pass we got to do some research and get the low-down so she can use it in her article for the website."

I worked as an Executive Assistant to the CEO of a start-up internet company based out of San Francisco called *Better Keep Jogging Baby* or better known by our website, www.bkjb.com. Our company was dedicated to providing fitness and nutrition information to the world.

"Spencer, you better or I will kick your ass when you get home and drag you to the gym with me on Tuesday morning." Ryan and I met our freshman year of college at UC Santa Cruz nine years ago when we were eighteen. Over the years I'd learned that her threats were really promises. She was *not* kidding.

"Alright, alright, I'll go pack my gym bag...after I finish this bowl of ice cream." Ryan rolled her eyes at me and I stuck my tongue out at her. I appreciated her support and enthusiasm, but I had never been a morning person and I wasn't about to start now.

My Monday workday dragged on and on, and all I wanted to do was go home, get in my PJs, and watch *The Voice*. When five o'clock rolled around, I honestly had half a mind to bypass the gym and do exactly that. But I remembered Ryan's threat, and I sure as shit didn't want her waking me up at 5:00 a.m. to go to the gym before work. Regardless, it was part of my job, and at least my boss had promised me extra vacation hours for doing this for her.

Alright, time to get this shit over with. Club 24 was an up and coming chain and I needed a new gym anyway. I used to go to the gym with my ex, Travis, or as Ryan liked to call him now, Trav*Ass*. I really hoped that I would never have to see him again, so thankfully this gym opened a little over a month ago and was close to work and home.

The gym was packed with the usual after-work crowd, but there were two treadmills open next to each other. Claiming one of them for myself, I popped in my iPod ear buds and started to walk briskly for my warm-up. Listening to music

4

while running always seemed to clear my head and right now I needed nothing but to let my mind go numb.

After running for five minutes, I thought I was going to pass out. I envisioned myself rolling off the treadmill like I had seen a few times on *The Biggest Loser*. That was all I needed with this packed gym. I slowed the treadmill back down to walk for a few minutes to catch my breath. Shortly after that, I noticed that someone had stepped onto the treadmill next to me.

I glanced to my right and that's when I noticed *him* for the first time. Trying not to get caught staring, I eyed him with my peripheral vision. Always a plus to have eye candy when you're doing something you really don't want to do. He was about six feet tall, appeared to be around my age of twenty-seven, had chestnut brown hair that was just long enough to have a messy spiky look, and broad shoulders... and oh wow—a smile that made my heart stop.

Of course, I was caught staring. *Shit.*

I reached for my phone and quickly texted Ryan.

Me: *OMFG, I have my very own Gideon Cross at the gym. Hot guy running on the treadmill next to me! :)*

Ryan: *Jealous! Don't tell Max, LOL...I want all the details TONIGHT.*

When I looked into the mirror in front of me, I noticed that my face was bright red. It was either from being exhausted on the treadmill or from being caught checking him out—probably a mixture of the two. After a few minutes of walking, I thought to myself, *Alright, you can't let this guy think you're that out of shape.* I sped back up to what I considered an energetic pace and started jogging again.

It had been at least a month since I had been to the gym. Before I discovered Trav*Ass* having a nooner with his secretary, Misty, we were in Hawaii. *What a sad cliché, right?* Little did I know that when Travis said he was getting texts from work, he really meant texts from Misty about what she couldn't wait to do to him when he was back home.

After another twenty minutes of jogging—and a few covert glances to my right—I couldn't take anymore. I stopped the treadmill and wiped it down. While backing off the treadmill, I peeked at *his* ass. *What a perfect ass...*Yep, my endorphins were flowing now. Taking a few steps towards the locker room, I glanced over my right shoulder to find him staring at me. *Holy shit.* Our eyes met and he gave me that heart-stopping smile he flashed when he first got on the treadmill. More a smirk than a smile, it still made my heart skip a beat.

Ryan was waiting for me when I walked into our house. "I ordered Chinese. It'll be here in ten. Go shower and then we can veg and you can tell me all about this *hottie.*"

"There isn't really much to tell."

"Anything is better than nothing. I have been with Max for three years. I need to live the single life vicariously through you now."

"Gee thanks," I said, and we both giggled.

After getting out of the shower, I smelled the aroma of the Chinese takeout Ryan had ordered. *Great, I just went to the gym and now I'm going to have a 3000 calorie meal.*

"What's on the menu tonight?" I asked as I walked into the kitchen and started opening the Chinese take-out boxes on the breakfast bar. Ryan's parents owned the house and rented it to us. They'd remodeled it for us as a graduation present and the kitchen was one of our favorite rooms. It was spacious and modern with stainless steel appliances and granite counter tops, but its white oak cabinets also gave it a homey feel.

"Only our favorites––Kung Pao Chicken, Broccoli Beef, Fried Rice and Cream Cheese Wontons."

Yep, that was an easy 3000 calories each. I gave an inward sigh.

"Alright, spill," Ryan demanded as she forked a piece of broccoli and bit into it with a crunch.

I paused to dip a Cream Cheese Wonton in sweet and sour sauce before stuffing it in my mouth. Savoring the creamy filling with a bit of tangy sweetness, I licked my fingers and sighed in contentment. "Like I said, there isn't much to say. I went to the gym and there was a total hottie running on the treadmill next to me."

"Well, what did he look like?"

I reached into the cabinet and grabbed a couple of wine glasses for us. Retrieving a bottle of chilled Moscato from the wine fridge, I poured a glass for each of us. I handed one to Ryan and we went to the living room and sat down on the floor by the coffee table. "Well, I'd say he's about six foot, around our age, with kind of short light brown hair...you know, just how I like them, and a smile...man, that smile makes me melt. I couldn't stare long enough to get a good look though. I just hope he is there again tomorrow."

Ryan continued to quiz me, but as I had told her repeatedly, I had been at the gym for less than an hour and hadn't even spoken to him. I had just snuck a few glances here and there. Well, hoped I snuck a few glances; I did get caught a few times.

After polishing off all of the food and watching a two hour episode of *The Voice*, I was beat. "Alright, I'm going to call it a night. I'll see you tomorrow when I get home from the gym," I said as I walked into the kitchen and put our dishes in the dishwasher.

"Wait, we forgot about our fortunes," Ryan said, tossing a fortune cookie to me.

Not only did we sometimes play the lotto numbers on the fortunes, but it was also tradition to add "in bed" at the end and giggle like little girls. "Oh right. What does yours say?" I asked as I cracked mine open.

"Courtesy is contagious... in bed."

"I bet Max would like that fortune for you," I said, laughing at her.

"I bet he would, too," she said, laughing as well. "What does yours say?"

"Be prepared to receive something special...in bed."

Ryan snatched the fortune out of my hand. "I bet that hottie at the gym has something to do with this!"

"Yeah right, I'm sure I will never see him again or get up the courage to talk to him."

"Uh huh. If you don't talk to him by the end of the week, I'm going down there."

Knowing Ryan and her threats, I hoped something did happen before she took control. It was also more motivation to get my ass to the gym. I had already decided that tomorrow I was going to go back and try the free kickboxing class they offered twice a week on Tuesdays and Thursdays.

Tuesday and Wednesday, I didn't see *him* when I went to the gym. I was starting to think that I never would get to see him again. But then I walked into the kickboxing class on Thursday night and there he was in the second row. I almost tripped over my own feet when I noticed him.

I was running a little late, so I stayed in the back of the class. Good thing, because it gave me the opportunity to stare at that perfect ass. About halfway through the class, the teacher told us to partner up so we could work on our abs by doing crunches.

I glanced up from beneath my lashes and he was looking at me with that smile I remembered from Monday. But he didn't make a move toward me and I didn't move toward him, though I badly wanted the guts to say something. Then the woman next to me offered to be my partner and I lost my chance.

While I was holding her legs, I glanced over and he was looking at me again. At least I thought he was. I casually glanced around to see who else he might be looking at, but the only other person it could have been was one of the guys who had partnered up on my right. Great––it'd be just my luck if he was gay.

After the class ended, I headed to the locker room. Just as I was about to enter, I heard a man's voice say "excuse me". My heart stopped. But when I turned around, it was only one of the guys who had been on my right side during crunches. "I think you forgot your towel." Disappointed that it wasn't my hottie who had stopped me, I thanked him as he handed my towel to me and then hurried into the locker room to change and head home.

〜

Friday night I headed straight home after work. It had been a long day and all I wanted was to take a long bath, heat up a Lean Cuisine and watch a chick flick.

I was halfway through *Serendipity* when Ryan stormed through the front door. She and Max always made Friday night "date night" and normally, she would spend the entire weekend at Max's place. "Hey, what are you doing home?" When I looked at her more closely and noticed that she had been crying, I quickly jumped up to give her a hug. "Oh my God, Ryan! What's wrong?"

Ryan accepted my hug and then took a minute to collect herself. Sitting down with me on the couch, she hugged her knees to her chest and tried her best to talk through her tears, her breath hitching every few words.

"Max and I went out to dinner and we started talking about getting married eventually – you know I've been hinting at a ring for months now. And then we were talking about what kind of house we'd buy together and how many rooms we'd need, and I said we'd need at least four bedrooms. Then he asked why we would need four bedrooms, because it's not like we were going to have kids or anything." Ryan had always pictured a life of living in the suburbs with a white picket fence, a loving husband, a dog and at least two kids. "And I said, 'What do you mean we're not having kids?' And he said that he works sixty-hour weeks and there was no way in hell he has time for babies. He just wants to spend his spare time with me and he'd rather be relaxing in Cabo than changing dirty diapers."

"I thought you and Max already talked about this and that he'd told you that he did want kids," I said, rubbing her back lightly to comfort her. "But hold that thought for just a sec. I'm grabbing some mint chocolate chip ice cream." I jumped up to grab the carton from the freezer and a spoon for each of us. We always kept the fridge stocked just in case we had a stressful day and this was always our go-to ritual for moments of crisis like this.

Ryan shoved a big bite of ice cream in her mouth before replying. "Well, apparently he changed his mind. Or he was just saying that to get me into bed. I don't know. But he said that he can't ever see himself being tied down with 'rugrats'."

"I'm so sorry, Ry. I know how much you really want kids. Maybe he will come around in time?"

"Fuck that, Spence, I broke up with him," she said angrily.

"You did what?" My mouth dropped open in shock.

"Why should I waste any more time on someone who doesn't want what I want?"

She was right, but she had just broken up with him, what, thirty minutes ago? And I knew she was madly in love with him, so no way had she given this decision enough thought.

"Don't you think that was maybe a little hasty? I mean, I know how much you love him and maybe he just needs a little time to get used to the idea that it's a deal breaker for you if he doesn't want to have kids. Give him a chance to change his mind or think about it more seriously. Maybe you could have tried going to counseling together?"

Ryan still looked furious, but then her shoulders slumped and she bit her lip uncertainly. "I don't know, Spence. Do you really think I fucked up by breaking up with him?"

I took another bite of ice cream and sighed. "I just know how good you guys are together and I think you could have put more effort into trying to work it out first."

"Maybe, but I was just so mad. It felt like he's just been lying to me all this time." Fresh tears burst into her eyes and she tossed her spoon on the coffee table.

Putting the ice cream down, I hugged her tightly again and pulled her up off the couch to march her to the bathroom. "What you need is a long, hot shower and then off to bed with you. You'll think more rationally and feel better in the morning after a good night's rest."

"Like I could sleep," she muttered, but she turned the shower on.

"Well, you know I am here for you if you need me," I said, and then closed the bathroom door.

A little while later after Ryan got out of the shower, I heard her go into her room. After my movie was over, I headed to my room. But first I stopped at Ryan's door, wanting to check on her. As I leaned my ear close to the door and heard her crying, my heart ached for her. Ryan had always been tough, but even tough people needed hugs. I wanted to go comfort her, but decided that I would let her have some alone time while she processed everything. In the morning, I would start my best friend therapy for her. I prayed to myself that they would eventually be able to talk things through and get back together because they were perfect for each other.

The next morning, I woke up early so I could cook us breakfast and make Ryan's favorite: chocolate chip pancakes and bacon. Just as the bacon was almost done, Ryan walked into the kitchen looking extremely depressed with puffy eyes from crying all night.

"Sit, I am making your favorites," I said to her as soon as she entered the kitchen.

"I'm not hungry."

"Too bad, I got up *early* just to make you a special breakfast."

"Fine, you know I can't pass up bacon."

"That's my girl." Setting her plate on the breakfast bar I said, "You know what? No more of us moping around thinking of the men in our life. Let's go to Vegas on Friday and enjoy a girl's trip!"

"Oh my God, Spence, let's do it!"

Ryan was always up for Vegas. I knew I didn't need to ask her twice. It was just the thing—we both needed a mini-vacation to process everything that had happened the last month with both of us. If Ryan still wanted Max back when we got home from Vegas, operation "Get Max Back" would be in full force.

CHAPTER TWO

The next week flew by. At the gym, I saw my hottie a few times, but he just smiled at me like he did every time he saw me. Maybe he was just being polite. I had already given up any hope that he would ask me out and I was way too chicken to say anything to him. Call me old fashioned, but the guy should make the first move. Besides, I'd given him plenty of flirtatious smiles to let him know I was interested and Ryan already forgot her threat because of the whole Max ordeal.

On Friday after work, Ryan and I headed to the airport. "I can't wait—long drunken nights followed by tanning by the pool during the day. This is going to be a blast," I said to Ryan.

"I know. What do you want to do first?"

"I don't know... let's see what clubs we can get into tonight with those free passes they give out on the Strip."

Ryan and I were no Vegas virgins. With it being only an hour and a half flight from SFO, we usually went to Vegas at least once or twice a year, or maybe more.

Just as Ryan and I approached our gate, I noticed him. My left arm and hand had a mind of their own as they launched out and grabbed Ryan's right arm. "Ow! What the hell, Spence?"

"Holy shit! The guy from the gym is sitting over there."

"Shut up! Oh my God, are you serious? Where? Which one?" Her head swung around to look for him.

"Dude, don't make it so obvious." I pinched her arm to make her stop looking. "Look casually...by the window between the guy and girl," I said while nudging my head in their direction. Of course, at that moment he decided to look up and caught me staring at him again. Without skipping a beat, he flashed me that heart-stopping smile. I felt like my legs were going to give out on me at any moment.

"*Damn!*" she said, dragging out the word. "He is *hot*, Spence. And I think he's going to Vegas, too."

"Seriously?" My pulse jumped as I thought of the possibility of us being seated next to each other on the plane.

"Well, it does look like he is waiting at our gate."

I was starting to feel a little giddy, but then I saw him smile and dip his head to listen to something the girl next to him was saying. *Please tell me that is not his girlfriend.* My heart began to sink.

I didn't know if being on the same flight was fate or pure coincidence, but it didn't matter if he was already taken. Regardless, I couldn't sit at the gate with him and kill myself wondering for the next hour. Sighing, I tugged on Ryan's arm. "Let's go grab a drink at the bar."

~

When we boarded the plane I saw him, but I wasn't sure if he noticed me since Ryan and I sat at the back of the plane and he was toward the front. I'm not sure what I would have done if we'd been seated close together.

If I wasn't so shy, I might have approached him and struck up a conversation. The last thing I'd expected upon arriving at the airport was finding him there, and I was certainly not expecting him to be on the same flight as me. I wondered where he was staying and why he was going to Vegas. And then scolded myself for wondering—none of that mattered if he had a girlfriend.

We landed in Vegas around eight. After about an hour, Ryan and I finally made it to our hotel. We spent the next hour getting ready to go out by freshening up our make-up and downing a bottle of champagne to get a head start on our night of partying. We decided to change into short skirts with sparkly tops and strappy high-heeled sandals that were sure to make our feet hurt from all the dancing. Looking in the mirror at ourselves and striking high fashion model poses, we giggled as we took one Facebook photo after another. Over the years we'd sometimes been mistaken as twins, but more often as sisters.

"Hey, what color eye shadow should I put on?" Ryan asked as she squeezed into the small bathroom where I was getting ready.

"I like the purple. It will bring out your brown eyes," I said, running the flat iron through my hair.

"Cool, what color are you going to wear?"

"I'm digging the silver."

"Oh, I like it. I think it will look good with your brown eyes and blue top."

"Yep, that is what I was thinking."

When we were ready, we set out to find a club. We knew that if we showed some skin, we would get a lot of attention from guys and hopefully score some free drinks. It's not like we were looking to hook up with random men or anything, but buying drinks in Vegas clubs was the fastest way to empty a girl's bank account. We just wanted to have a good time, dance and hopefully not have too bad of a hangover the next morning.

We walked down the Strip soaking in what some people called "Disneyland for Adults". It had been a while since Ryan and I had last been to Vegas, and we were like little kids in a candy shop.

We finally found a guy who was passing out club passes. He handed us two for Lavo at The Palazzo. Thankfully, we were able to skip the long line and get in for free. When we made it into the club, I gave Ryan a little booty bump with my hip and grinned at her—it was gorgeous inside.

The bar was packed, but I was finally able to nudge my way between people and ordered two redheaded sluts. "I'm going to need at least one more of these before I am able to get on the dance floor," I yelled so Ryan could hear me over the loud music, and she nodded in agreement.

We quickly drank our shots and I turned around to order another round, but the bartender handed me two more before I said a word. "This is from the gentleman over there." He nodded towards the other end of the bar, "The one in the black shirt." I quickly turned my head to see what nice guy had bought us a drink. Of course it was *him.*

I turned back to Ryan, slapping her arm to get her attention. "Holy shit, Mr. Hottie just bought us a drink!"

"Who?" she said, as she scanned the room.

"The guy from the gym. What do I do? Oh my God, what do I say? Maybe he doesn't have a girlfriend after all." I was starting to freak out a little. He bought me a drink—I had to make the first move to talk to him. *Alright Spencer, time to put your big girl panties on.*

I turned to go over to thank him but he was gone. *What the fuck?* He was there one second and gone the next. Was he some sort of ninja? I swear he was just standing there. I scanned the room that was packed to the brim, but I didn't see him.

My face fell. "Ahh Ryan... I think he left."

She shrugged. "Weird. Oh well. Drink up so we can dance."

We clicked our glasses with a quick cheer, threw our shots back and made our way onto the dance floor. The dance floor was lightly lit with colorful strobe lights surrounded by cushioned booths on the outside edges.

We had been dancing for at least a half hour with different people; sometimes a group of girls, sometimes some guys. I was just about to leave the dance floor for a quick break to rest my tired feet when I felt someone start dancing with me from behind. Whoever it was placed their hands on my hips. As buzzed as I was, I didn't really think anything of it and continued to dance. About a minute later, Ryan turned to say something to me. Her eyes grew big and in that moment I realized who I must be dancing with.

Desire overtook my emotions. I had waited almost three weeks for his touch. Fantasized about it a few nights when all I could do was think of him and his smile when I tried to fall asleep at night.

The music pounded in my head. His arms wrapped around my waist from behind, pulling me against him. I could feel the hard muscles of his chest against my back. His hips moved against mine. With his hard length pressing into my ass, I could feel how much he wanted me. I wanted him just as badly.

Jeremih's hit *Down on Me* featuring 50 Cent played as our bodies moved with the music. I reached up with my right hand and held onto the back of his neck and slid my fingers through his hair. He pulled me harder against his erection. It felt like the whole club had disappeared. All I could do now was close my eyes and enjoy the ride that I had longed for.

Our hips rocked and popped to the song. Just like the song was saying, I was grinding my ass into him. I felt his face bury in my hair as he kissed my neck lightly sending tingles down my entire body. Moisture starting to build between my legs. My heart started beating faster and my breath caught.

The strobe lights flashed over the dance floor, reflecting off a rotating disco ball as the beat of the music thumped in my ears. It felt like we were dancing for hours. Everything seemed to be in slow motion; however, Jeremih and 50 were still singing.

Just as the song ended the DJ started playing the next song. It was one of my new favorites, a remix of Alex Clare's song, *Too Close*.

He spun me around so his right leg fit snugly between my legs. He looked down at me, his mocha colored eyes locked with mine. I wrapped my arms around his neck and ran my fingers through his hair again, loving the silky texture. He slid his hands down my back and cupped my ass as we rocked, swayed and gyrated to the pounding music.

My skirt was very short, so it was slowly sliding up my thighs which gave the front of my panties contact with his jean-clad thigh. My heart raced more as my panties dampened and my clit throbbed with an almost painful need for more. His fingers tightened against my ass as he pulled me harder against his leg. Sweat rolled down my back—it was almost too much.

He was grinding his thigh against my clit as I thought of how badly I'd wanted him for weeks. I was *finally* dancing with him—though I still didn't even know his name. But in the midst of my thoughts and the overwhelming feeling of touching him and dancing with him, I couldn't have stopped my climax even if I'd wanted to. I couldn't believe the intensity of the feelings I was experiencing there in public with him, surrounded by people.

I tugged tighter onto his hair while trying not to collapse from the surge of pleasure running all the way through me. I leaned my head into his chest to muffle the moan that escaped my mouth as I climaxed. I tried to stop dancing to enjoy the orgasm, but his hands grasped my ass tighter as he kept me pressed hard against his leg so our bodies continued to sway to the music.

If he had asked me to go up to his room at that moment, I would have said yes. I had never hooked up with a stranger, let alone in Vegas...at a club. I had never had sex in public, never had an orgasm in public for that matter. I didn't care.

At last, we slowly stopped dancing, but he was still pulling me hard onto his leg and his eyes were locked with mine. He gave me his smile that I remembered so well. I was trying to relax and let my heart return to normal, but looking into his eyes only made it race more. I still couldn't speak— could barely breathe. A few seconds later, the song ended. He bent down, nuzzled my neck and I could feel his warm breath against my cheek as he whispered, "Thank you," and then walked away.

CHAPTER THREE

Thank you? What the fuck just happened? I stood there stunned for what seemed like an eternity. Ryan stepped in front of me. "Oh my God, Spence, that was the fucking hottest dancing I have ever seen!"

"I need a drink...maybe even a cigarette." I had never smoked before but it seemed appropriate at the moment. Ryan and I made our way back to the bar. I really needed to sit down for a minute. I squeezed between people to get the bartender's attention again and ordered four shots of *Patron*. Ryan and I sat long enough to toss our shots back like champs. We were feeling really, really good. I was definitely on Cloud Nine if not Cloud One Hundred!

After a quick restroom break to do a mirror check, we resumed our dancing out on the dance floor. I only danced with Ryan the rest of the night, a little bummed that he didn't dance with me again. I wasn't even sure if he was still there as I didn't see him again. I kept replaying our two dances over and over in my head.

It was getting close to the wee hours of the morning. I tapped Ryan's shoulder, "Ry, it's time for bed." I was beat. I'd worked a full day before we left for Vegas, and considering that my brain was a cluster fuck at that moment, I was in dire need of my bed. Ryan agreed and we decided to call it a night as we headed back to our room.

⌒〜

The next day, Ryan and I ate brunch at Café Vettro at the Aria hotel where we were staying. Realizing we had drunk our dinner last night, we were both starving. After brunch, we decided to go to the Liquid Day Club & Lounge at our hotel. It had two pools for adults only, which was perfect for us. No way did I want to spend the day with screaming kids running around. There were private cabanas and chaise lounge chairs to enjoy while listening to the DJ play the latest hits. The lounge also provided a full bar that had a light food menu. Ryan and I were set for the day.

Enjoying the desert sun in the middle of September was perfect. Just as I was drifting off to sleep on the chaise lounge, two guys made their way to us. "Hello ladies. I'm Trevor and this is my friend Matt--we were wondering if we could buy you pretty ladies a drink?" Of course Ryan and I were not going to pass up a free drink.

Ryan spoke up first, "Yes, you may! I'm Megan and this is my friend Courtney." We greeted each other with a handshake. I wasn't expecting Ryan to remember our "Vegas" names. We used the names when we had no interest in the men that we encountered. It wasn't that Matt and Trevor were sleazebags, but Ryan and I were not in the habit of picking up random guys out of town.

Matt and Trevor were both tall with athletic builds and looked gorgeous in their swim trunks. They had mouth-watering chiseled abs, bare chests and huge biceps. However, neither one of them were my type. They both had surfer blond hair and blue eyes, but I preferred brown hair and brown eyes, like *him.*

Of course there was nothing wrong with the way Matt and Trevor looked. Ryan and I would definitely pretend to be into them. Actually Ryan wouldn't even have to pretend as they were both her type. I just had someone else on my mind.

Matt and Trevor bought us a drink and we spoke about what our plans for the night were. At that moment we had no idea. Matt and Trevor told us that we should check out the club at Aria called Haze. We thought it was a good idea since it was in our hotel. After an hour of chatting, Ryan and I said our goodbyes to Matt and Trevor and told them that we might see them later at the club.

$\sim$

It was starting to get late in the afternoon and Ryan wanted to go shopping. After getting ready, we shopped all along the Strip. We went to the Miracle Mile at Planet Hollywood, window shopped at the Venetian and strolled through the shops at the Bellagio.

Ryan spent a pretty penny, but I didn't see anything I wanted until we passed by *Louis Vuitton* at the Bellagio. "I have always wanted a Louis," I said longingly. Ryan grew up with a privileged life, while I was raised in the average middle-income family. So while she was always able to shop at all the high end designer boutiques, I had always bought my clothes and purses at Target. And I still loved Target, but it wasn't *Louis Vuitton*.

"Why don't you buy one? You haven't bought anything all day but food." Ryan didn't understand the concept of living paycheck to paycheck. Not only did her family have money, but she made more money than me. Heck, if I wasn't living with Ryan at one of her parent's houses, I would probably be living in a one bedroom apartment that was six hundred square feet for twenty-five hundred dollars a month.

"I can't afford a two-thousand dollar purse!" I said, laughing at Ryan's frivolous suggestion. "Come on, let's go eat and then get ready to go to that club, Haze."

Later that night, we made our way downstairs to Haze. While it was packed and had dimmed lighting, Matt and Trevor seemed to spot us quickly. They bought us drinks again and asked us to dance. I danced with Trevor while Ryan danced with Matt. Ryan seemed to be enjoying herself as Matt was very attentive and never left her side throughout the night.

However, Trevor danced a little too close for my comfort and all I could think about was my previous night dancing with my hottie. But they kept buying us drinks, and Ryan was having such a good time and finally seemed to have gotten her mind off of Max for a while, so I figured the least we could do was dance with them.

It was starting to get pretty late...or should I say early in the morning. Ryan and I decided to call it a night. Before leaving, Matt and Trevor asked for our phone numbers. They said they lived in Tacoma, Washington and could easily come see us in Seattle. Ryan and I had mentioned earlier at the pool that we were from Seattle. We both knew how to play the part of Megan and Courtney because we had done it several times over the years. We gave them our fake phone numbers and told them we hoped we would hear from them soon.

While on our way back to our room, I told Ryan that I wanted to put my last six dollars that I had in my pocket in a slot machine. We stopped at one of the *Lucky 7* machines. I put my six dollars in, pressed the max bet of three dollars...nothing. I pressed the max bet button again and the first row hit a Wild 7 followed by the second row hitting another Wild 7. The third row continued to spin for what seemed like forever. I held my breath and... it hit another Wild 7! My heart stopped and Ryan and I both started jumping up and down, waving our hands and "woo-hooing" while the bell on the machine rang. I had hit the jackpot!

After all the commotion ended, the slot attendant came over to pay me out. I thought I had hit the jackpot for thousands, but in reality, the jackpot was only eight hundred and fifty five dollars.

"Spence, you should go play Texas Hold'em and try to win the other half for your Louis!"

"I don't know… maybe I'll just save it." Ryan's idea sounded tempting, but I wasn't sure. I had just won and now had eight hundred and fifty five dollars and that was a lot more than I came with.

"Come on, Spence, I have seen you take your family for all their money at Thanksgiving multiple times and you play all the time online."

Of course, Ryan was right. I was just nervous. I had never played with *real* people before. "Fine, let's go." What did I really have to lose?

While we headed towards the Poker Room, I noticed the High Roller Room. Might as well go big or go home right? We walked into the High Roller room instead and I stopped dead in my tracks, causing Ryan to plow into me from behind. "Ow, whoa Spence, why did you stop?"

I gave Ryan the head nudge towards my left. *He* was sitting at the table. Her eyes widened, but she didn't say anything and neither did I.

I nervously sat down at the one empty seat that was on the end directly across from *him*. He was sitting with the guy and girl I had seen him with at the airport. When I sat down, his eyes lit up and there was that slow, sexy smile again.

The dealer took my money and gave me eight hundred and fifty five dollars worth of chips. Since the table had a one hundred dollar open, I potentially could only play eight hands if I didn't win any hands and no one raised it pre-flop.

In Texas Hold'em, every player is dealt two cards face down. Everyone who wants to play places a bet and everyone who doesn't want to play folds by giving their cards back to the dealer. After everyone puts in their chips and either matches the big blind (also known as an ante) or matches the highest raise, the dealer burns one card (also known as discarding) and then turns three over which is known as the flop. Everyone either bets or folds again, and then the dealer burns one card and turns another over which is known as the turn. Once everyone has bet or folded again, the dealer burns one last card and then turns over one final card which is known as the river. Everyone who is still playing bets or folds again, and then you turn over your cards to see who has the highest hand.

Since the big blind was a hundred dollars and the small blind was fifty, I thought to myself that this was probably a bad idea. But now that *he* was here, I was glued to my seat.

I didn't play my first hand. I was dealt a seven of clubs and a two of diamonds. I knew enough to know that a seven-two was the worst hand in poker. *Great, is this how this is going to go?* I looked up and he gave me a smile that I interpreted as *Hey I know what you did last night!* I felt my face start to heat as I remembered the details of that night all too clearly.

While the dealer dealt the next hand, his friend turned to me and started to introduce himself and his friends. "Hi, I'm Jason, this is my wife Becca, and this here is Brandon," he said, nodding towards my hottie. The older gentleman sitting at the table introduced himself as Stan but didn't know Brandon and his friends. Finally he had a name and the woman he was with was not his girlfriend. I was relieved. When we'd danced, I hadn't thought once about the possible girlfriend I'd seen him with at the airport.

"Hi, I'm Spencer and this is Ryan." Since I knew Brandon went to my gym, I didn't feel that I should give him our fake names... especially after that dance and since I wanted to get to know him. God, did I want to get to know this *gorgeous* man!

"So ladies, where are you from?" From the tone of Jason's question, I knew he already knew the answer.

"San Francisco. And you?" Two could play this game.

"Wow, what a coincidence. So are we," Jason said, answering my question.

"You know, you look like this girl who goes to the same gym as me," Brandon said as he looked into my eyes, making my palms grow sweaty.

"Oh yeah? I just started going to that new gym, Club 24, a few weeks ago... You know, come to think of it, you do look kind of familiar." Our eyes were locked on each other and he flashed me his smile. We both knew who each other was, but I kept playing his game.

"Yeah, then I know I have seen you a few times there," Brandon said with his knowing eyes.

Over the next hour, we all made small talk, talking about San Francisco and why we were in Vegas. Ryan, with her big mouth, explained to everyone that I was playing poker because I had just hit a jackpot on a slot machine and I wanted to try to double my money for a *Louis Vuitton* purse. *Thanks Ryan. Now I was thoroughly embarrassed.*

Brandon and I caught each other staring throughout the wee hours of the night. We didn't mention the previous night once. But he gave me his signature heart-stopping smile frequently.

I was winning most hands I played, and I thought that I was about to reach two thousand dollars. The next hand, the dealer dealt me pocket kings. Being a strong starting hand, I raised pre-flop to four hundred dollars. Wow, that was like a fourth of my rent. Everyone folded except Brandon.

On the flop, the dealer turned over a king of clubs, ace of diamonds and a two of spades. *Three of a kind, not bad.* I swallowed hard, trying to maintain my poker face and then I bet five hundred dollars. Brandon called. The dealer turned over an eight of spades on the turn. No help to me. I bet another five hundred dollars and Brandon called again. The dealer then turned over a seven of hearts on the river which again was no help to me.

Knowing that a three of a kind was a strong hand and there was no chance for a straight or a flush, I pushed all my chips in the middle and said "All in." Brandon looked up at me and flashed me that smile that I was already falling in love with. I knew I was in trouble.

"I call," he said. The dealer counted all the chips I had put in the middle which totaled one thousand six hundred and fifty dollars. I was nervous. I couldn't believe I had just bet all that money. My heart started to beat fast and my palms were sweaty. This was it. I could either win enough for my purse or go home empty-handed.

I turned over my pocket kings revealing I had a three of a kind. Still smiling, Brandon turned over pocket aces. *Shit! Of course*. Brandon also had a three of a kind, but it was aces and that beat my kings.

I was stunned. What are the odds? "Ah Spence, you lost all your money!" Ryan said mournfully. *No shit Sherlock!*

"Yep, well it was nice playing with you all," I said as I stood up. "Time to call it a night, Ry." I was extremely disappointed, but at least I'd finally met Brandon officially.

Ryan and I turned to leave, but stopped when Brandon spoke. "Hey Spencer..."

I hesitated for a slight moment then turned. "Yeah?"

Smiling, Brandon said, "See you at the gym on Monday."

"Okay," I said with a huge smile on my face. I probably looked like a complete idiot as I grinned from ear to ear, but I didn't care. Vegas had turned out to be everything I wished for and more.

Ryan and I walked out of the room and there were butterflies in my stomach. As soon as we got out of earshot range—at least I hoped we were—we did a little victory dance and jumped up and down. The hottie at the gym finally talked to me. Unlike Vegas' slogan, not everything stays in Vegas––thank God!

Ryan and I made it home from Vegas on Sunday afternoon. We were both exhausted; partying all weekend really took a lot out of us. We ordered pizza and lounged in our PJs for the evening as we'd already decided it was going to be an early night for both of us. "Are you nervous about seeing Brandon tomorrow?" Why did Ryan always seem to ask the obvious questions?

"*Um, yes.*" God was I nervous. It would be the first time we were "alone" together after Vegas and our dance. I had no idea what was going to happen.

I tossed and turned all night because my brain would just not shut off.

The next day, work progressed as a normal Monday; very slow and I thought it would never end. Finally, at five, I made my way to the gym. My guest pass was expired, so I had to buy a membership.

When I got to the front desk, there was a person in front of me. While waiting, I looked around, but I didn't see Brandon. Finally it was my turn. "Hi, I need to purchase a membership," I said to the guy at the front desk.

Before he had a chance to respond, I heard Brandon say from behind me, "Luke, I'm taking care of Spencer's membership."

"Yes sir, Mr. Montgomery," Luke said.

Just then, Brandon was on my right leaning on the desk. I quickly sized him up and down. He was dressed in black basketball shorts and a dark blue tank top that clung to what looked like perfect abs and what I knew was a rock hard chest. His biceps were big but not too big. He was perfect. "That isn't necessary," I said to Brandon.

"It's the least I can do for taking all your money!" he said with laughter in his voice.

"Ha ha, very funny. But really, you don't need to. It was just money I won in Vegas anyway, so no big deal."

"Spencer, don't worry about it, I kind of own this place."

"What? Really?" I wasn't expecting him to say that, I'd just thought we went to the same gym, not that I went to *his* gym!

"Yep, now go change so we can work out," he said, his tone a little bossy, but I liked it.

I hurried and changed. Brandon was waiting for me when I exited the locker room. "Ready?" he asked.

"Yep." We walked over to the treadmills. Again, this reminded me of a scene in one of my favorite books. If every work day ended like this, I might never retire.

After running on the treadmill for twenty minutes and sharing those flirty glances, Brandon asked me if I wanted to go to the weight room. I had never lifted weights before because I thought I needed to do cardio only. I didn't want to be bulky like a man, but he assured me that I needed both. Who was I to argue? He was, in fact, the owner of the gym, so I figured that meant he knew his stuff.

In the weight room, he showed me some basic exercises. While I was concentrating on trying not to pull a muscle, he was working on his triceps. He was leaning backwards on a weight bench with his legs stretched out in front of him while doing backwards pushups. It was then that I saw the sexiest thing I had ever seen. Not all men have it, but when they do, it made my mouth water. People refer to it as "the horseshoe". It's where the tricep is so defined, it makes a horseshoe shape on the back of your arm when the muscle flexes.

Just as I started to lick my lips, Brandon looked up at me. "You like what you see?" *Fuck, did I ever!*

"Uh huh..." was all I could muster out of my mouth.

"Good," he said with a wink.

After we were done in the weight room, Brandon walked me back to the locker room. "What are you doing tomorrow night after the gym?" he asked.

Not wanting to seem over eager, I pretended to think for a moment, then casually said, "I don't really have any plans."

"Would you like to have dinner with me after we work out?"

"Sure, I would love to," I said, smiling at him. "I'll see you tomorrow." I turned and walked into the locker room.

～

When I got home, Ryan was in the living room watching TV. She started to grill me about my night at the gym.

"So tell me. Did you kiss?"

"While working out at the gym?"

"He could have cornered you in the ladies locker room."

"I wish!"

"So what did *you* do?"

"First of all, Brandon has the sexiest body I have ever seen!"

"You didn't kiss, but you had sex?"

48

"What? *No!* But I can just tell. While he was lifting weights, he had the horseshoe on his triceps for crying out loud!"

"Wow, that is sexy," she agreed with a wistful sigh.

"I know, right? Also, he owns the gym."

"Holy shit! Really?"

"Yep, and he took care of my membership."

"Ah, I am so jealous of you right now, Spencer," Ryan said as she slouched down on the couch.

"I know. I can't believe this is happening. Oh, and we are going to dinner tomorrow after work."

"I hate you," Ryan said quietly and crossed her arms over her chest.

"No, you don't."

"Yes, I do!" We both laughed. Ryan was never really good at hiding her jealousy.

CHAPTER FOUR

The next day at the gym, Brandon joined me for the Tuesday kickboxing class. The instructor gave us a weird look when we entered the class. I thought for a second that maybe it was because the owner of the gym was in her class but then I remembered he was in here last week, too. This time during crunches we partnered up right away.

After I did my set of fifty crunches we switched positions so he could do his set. I had my hands on his feet to hold them down as my face leaned close to his bent knees. His basketball shorts slid up his leg a little exposing his thick muscular thigh.

When he was on number forty nine, Brandon crunched up and quickly brushed his lips with mine, taking me by surprise. He did the same with number fifty and it took everything I had to not straddle him in the crowded class and return the kiss but for much longer. I was starting to really enjoy working out again.

After the class, I went to the locker room to shower and get ready for dinner. I had brought my clothes so I didn't have to waste time running home to get ready.

I dressed in a simple navy blue a-line dress that fell loosely above my knees. The dress was sleeveless with ruffles down the front. I accented the dress with a rope braided belt, snake skin wedge heels and a ruffle clutch purse, all cream colored. Given that I didn't want to keep Brandon waiting, I quickly blew-dry my hair and put in my go-to princess cut diamond stud earrings.

When I exited the locker room, Brandon was leaning on the wall outside the door waiting patiently for me. He was dressed in dark denim jeans, and a black pinstripe long sleeve button down shirt with his hair a little spiked, but in the messy just-fucked look, and he smelled like the fresh air mixed with warm sunshine, the ruggedness of the earth and all man. I still couldn't place his cologne even though I had smelled it before.

"Hey, beautiful," Brandon said as he caught his first glimpse of me coming out of the locker room. "Wow, you're breathtaking."

"Thank you, you're not too bad yourself." I was blushing.

He placed his hand on the small of my back, sending a shiver of excitement down my spine. We walked out of the gym toward the parking lot and he directed me to his silver *Range Rover Sport* that was parked in one of the two "Reserved" parking spots right outside the front doors. Being very chivalrous, Brandon came around and opened the passenger side door. While he walked around to the driver's side, I took in the sleek all black leather interior with chrome accents. It felt very masculine to me.

"Cold? Would you like me to turn on the seat warmers?" Brandon said as he slid into the car.

"What? Your car has butt warmers?" I said with a chuckle.

"Yes, we do live in the Bay Area."

There was no argument there. San Francisco seemed to have more foggy days than sunny days year round. There were maybe a few weeks out of the summer months that were perfect;

not too warm and not too hot. The nights were always chilly though.

"I would love my butt warmed!" I said with a big grin on my face. After all, I was in a dress.

"I'll have to remember that."

"Where are we going for dinner," I asked, smiling at his comment as he pulled out of the lot. Michael Buble's song *Home* was playing quietly in the background.

"Do you like seafood? I was thinking we could go to Scoma's in Sausalito."

"I love seafood. That sounds perfect."

There was also a Scoma's that was only a few minutes from the gym. I figured Brandon wanted as much time with me like I wanted with him. As we made our way out of San Francisco towards Sausalito, Brandon reached over and laced his fingers with mine, gently stroking his thumb over the back of my hand. The Golden Gate Bridge was lit up with golden lights as the sun was setting behind clouds that started to roll in.

"Did you guys have fun in Vegas?" I asked.

"Let's just say Vegas was... unforgettable," he said with a huge grin that made me blush. "I've never been a huge fan of 50 Cent before, but I have to say I am a new believer." My face was fully beet red as I concentrated furiously on the dashboard in front of me. "But how did you know it was me?"

I turned toward him with my face still beet red. "Ryan and I have been friends forever. The look she gave me said it all."

"Well I was considering myself lucky I didn't get a knee in the groin. But when I saw you dancing there, all sexy and confident, I couldn't stop myself."

"I wouldn't dance with just anyone like *that*." He was making me feel warm all the way down to the tips of my toes as I just sat there grinning like an idiot. I couldn't help it.

"So did you and Ryan have fun the rest of your trip?"

"Yeah, much needed girl time. She's getting over her ex and it's still pretty recent. How much money did you end up winning at the poker table?"

"After I took *your* money, I then took Stan for two thousand. After that, we called it a night since it was just Jason, Becca and myself left at the table...so I walked away with about four grand."

"*Damn* that's a lot."

"Yep, not too bad. Jason made me buy them an early breakfast before we headed for bed though."

After the twenty or so minute drive, we pulled into downtown Sausalito driving past the restaurant to find parking. Almost to the end of Bridgeway where Scoma's was located on a small pier, we found an open spot.

Brandon and I got out of his car and started to walk toward the restaurant. He reached down and grabbed my hand again, which made me smile. It had been a long time since I had been on a first date. I was so nervous that I had butterflies in my stomach.

Scoma's is built on a little pier over the San Francisco Bay. Brandon had reserved a table by the window for us. Even though it was a cloudy evening and looked like it could rain at any time, the view was absolutely beautiful. I ordered the Scallops Parmigano and Brandon ordered the Sesame Ahi Tuna and a bottle of the *2011 Groth Sauvignon Blanc* from a local winery in Napa.

"So, how long have you lived in San Francisco?" Brandon asked after the waiter had taken our order.

"Ryan and I moved here right after college... so it's been about five years. What about you?"

"Jason, Becca and I moved here from Austin about a year and a half ago. We all went to *Texas A&M*."

"What was your Major?"

"Well, I received a full ride scholarship for football, but I was injured my sophomore year and wasn't able to continue with my goal of a career in professional football. I never played again. I concentrated more on my academics and Jason and I graduated with Bachelor Degrees in Business Administration."

"Wow, how were you injured?"

"Um, it's a long story; I'll save it for another time."

"Okay, well, what made all three of you move out here?"

"After college, Jason and I opened a gym in Austin, and it was so successful that we decided to open one in Houston, where I'm from. Then we opened a third in Denver when an opportunity arose for us to buy a gym that was going out of business. After that, we were ready for a change of scenery and to get out of the humidity and really wanted to open a gym on the west coast, so we decided to move out here to San Francisco. It's much easier to concentrate on getting a business up and running when you live in the same town. It was more difficult when we were managing Houston and Denver and living in Austin."

"I've always wanted to go to Texas. I would like to someday see the Alamo."

"Maybe I can take you sometime," he said smiling, making me blush.

"Sounds like fun."

The waiter returned and expertly poured our glasses of wine and left warm bread on the table with butter. I felt my stomach growl as I realized I hadn't eaten since lunch time.

"You know, when I first saw you at the gym, I wanted to talk to you. I even managed to get close to you while you ran on the treadmill, but I couldn't get my courage up to talk to you. Plus, I was still kind of seeing someone at the time, and it wouldn't have been fair to you or her."

"Yeah, I didn't have the balls, either." *Shit, did that just come out of my mouth?* We both laughed.

"Christy, the girl I was seeing, and I didn't really have anything in common. She became extremely lazy over the few months we dated, quit her job because she was bored, questioned my every move, every phone call and text and hated Jason." Apparently Jason was not too fond of her either.

"I finally ended it with Christy a week before Vegas. Again, I wanted to talk to you, but I figured it was too soon. Then I saw you at the airport, which caught me off guard. Before I could walk over to you, you were gone. When I saw you and Ryan at Lavo that night, I knew I just had to talk to you. Except after we danced, I could barely get two words out of my mouth," Brandon said with a chuckle.

I was surprised at that. He seemed so cool, calm and collected – so self-assured and confident. I could hardly speak after we danced and had needed two shots of tequila to calm my nerves.

"I'm sorry I left like that. I just had to get back to my room and...you know, take a cold shower." Brandon's face was slightly flushed, so I could only imagine that my own face must have been bright red at that moment.

"I was really happy I ended it with Christy before Vegas–-it was a long time coming. Thankfully, I got to know you a little better in Vegas and here we are."

"I'm happy, too. One more night with no new information for Ryan and I think she would have been to the gym on Monday to kick your ass for not making a move!"

The waiter returned with our entrees as the sun set fully behind darkened clouds. Looking across the bay, I saw slight flickers of lights from the small town of Belvedere. Over the course of dinner we talked about hobbies, likes, dislikes, favorite movies, etc.-- everything you would ask on a first date. I found out that he liked to go mountain bike riding with his friends, hated broccoli, his favorite food was barbeque ribs and his favorite movie of all time was *Tommy Boy* with Chris Farley.

He loved sports; his favorite baseball team was our local team, the *San Francisco Giants*, favorite hockey team was also our local team, the *San Jose Sharks,* and his favorite football team was the *Dallas Cowboys.* I wasn't sure I was ready to tell him about Trav*Ass*, so I quickly told him that I had just gotten out of a two year relationship and didn't elaborate further than that. He didn't press me for more information, but continued to listen attentively as I went on to tell him that I loved all the sports teams he mentioned except for the football team. I was a *San Francisco Forty Niners* fan.

Brandon had an extra ticket for Friday's Giants game and we made plans for me to go with him, Jason and Becca. I was nearly giddy again; thrilled that he seemed to want to spend more time with me. I had missed the feeling of new relationship butterflies in my stomach and I loved how I could sit here for hours and talk with Brandon. It was odd how comfortable I already felt with him.

Thinking back to my first date with Trav*Ass*, it had been rather awkward. Even though I was instantly attracted to him, the conversation didn't flow like it did with Brandon. There was a lot of dead silence. But with Brandon, no such problem existed -- our conversation flowed like we had known each other for years.

All too soon though it started to get a little late and Brandon had an early meeting the next morning. We were about to leave the restaurant when we noticed that a downpour of rain had just started. Neither one of us had brought an umbrella. Come to think of it, the weather man did say it was going to rain this evening, but they were never right...except this time.

"Want to make a break for it, or do you want me to go get the car?"

61

Not wanting to seem too much like a girl, I said, "Let's make a break for it, a little water won't hurt."

Brandon smiled, took my hand, and we were out the door running. Drenched with rain drops, we finally made it to the car. Brandon opened my door first and then he ran around the front of the car and got in himself.

"Whoa, it is really coming down! I have a few gym towels in here somewhere," he said as he reached in the backseat to find them. He handed me a towel and turned the car on, then turned the heater and "butt warmers" on. I was starting to shiver from being wet and cold.

I was drying myself off when Brandon reached over to help me. "Here, this one is dry," he said as he started to dry my left leg with the dry towel in his hands. His touch sparked a desire deep in my stomach. I grabbed his hand to stop him from drying my leg and looked into his eyes, our faces close together. I leaned over and kissed him lightly.

I started to pull away after realizing what I had done. Brandon dropped the towel he was using to dry my leg, grabbed the back of my head and kissed me harder. With our mouths still locked and tongues exploring each other's mouth, I pushed him back and climbed over the center console to straddle him. My back was pressed uncomfortably against the steering wheel, but I barely noticed. I cupped my hands on his shaved cheeks while his hands ran up and down my smooth legs and my skin tingled from only his touch. I could feel the wetness from his rain-dampened jeans on my bare skin under my dress.

His stiff erection was pressed into my left thigh. Flashes of us dancing filled my head and I moaned. He moved his warm hands farther up my legs and cupped my ass under my dress, only the thin material of my panties separating his fingers from my skin. Breaking our mouths free, I trailed my lips down his jaw until they reached his neck. His skin was just a bit salty as I licked lightly over his rapidly beating pulse, all the while rubbing myself harder against his bulging cock. I had never been so forward before in my life. Brandon just had that effect on me. He was by far the best kisser I'd ever had and it was like my body craved him——I just couldn't get enough.

From my backside, I felt his fingers slip into my panties. My pulse jumped and sped up as I paused my kiss, the anticipation almost as exciting as I knew his touch would be. His fingers lightly caressed me, toying with my sensitive outer-lips and I moaned again. "Fuck, you're so wet!" Brandon whispered into my ear, his breath warm against my skin.

"Well, we did just run through the rain," I said breathlessly.

"That's not what I meant," he said with a smile, then took my lips again. His mouth was hot and his tongue dueled with mine as his tongue mimicked the motion of his fingers on the sensitized skin of my pussy. My stomach clenched with excitement.

Straightening my spine, I tilted my head back as Brandon grabbed a fistful of my hair with his left hand, tilting my head back even further. He ran light kisses over my neck while adjusting his hand to insert two fingers in my pussy.

Another moan escaped my mouth when his fingers filled me. His fingers felt so good inside of me and he rubbed his thumb over my clit. Suddenly I felt a vibration on my right leg. Realizing it was Brandon's phone ringing, I said, "Do you need to get that?" I pulled my head back, looking into his eyes.

"No, it can't be that important. I'll call them back," he said, returning his mouth to mine. Rain danced all over the car, the windows fogging as it mixed with our body heat and the car's heater. Brandon's lips felt so good on mine that I wanted to stay and kiss him forever.

My hands skimmed over his hard biceps and the firmness of his chest and torso. I moved my hand and traced the buttons of his shirt as I slid it up so I could feel his smooth chiseled abs. His fingers enticed all my right spots while his thumb continued to circle over my clit. I felt my body getting close to climaxing. I bent my head to run feather kisses down his neck and began running my hands through his soft hair as my body started to shatter. Continuing to ride his fingers, I flicked my tongue over his neck and then bit it lightly.

When Brandon removed his fingers, we sat holding each other. I didn't want to leave. He reached around me shutting off the car and cracked his window a little. "It's getting a little hot in here."

"A little?" I was drenched from the rain and from our heated passion.

After a few minutes, he gently took my chin, tilted it up and lightly kissed me. "Time to get you home."

I climbed back into my seat and buckled my seatbelt while Brandon inched his car out onto the street. I was concentrating on slowing my heartbeat and calming myself down again.

Brandon looked over at me with a smirk, "So you're a biter?"

CHAPTER FIVE

It had stopped raining by the time we pulled up to my house. Brandon walked me to my front door and kissed me good night. "I'll see you tomorrow at the gym," he said while turning to leave.

"*Details*!" Ryan demanded as soon as my foot entered the door. I told her all about my night but discreetly left out a few of the after dinner details.

"How was your night?" I asked, quickly changing the subject. Ryan said she had spent the evening watching *The Voice* while eating leftover pizza from Sunday night. I could tell that she was still depressed. I needed to get her out of her funk but needed some time to come up with my "Get Max Back" plan.

"Tomorrow when I get home from the gym, you want to go out to dinner and drinks? Maybe Karaoke at The Mint?"

"No."

"What? Why not?"

"I just want to sit here and watch TV."

"Oh no you don't. Remember that was me two weeks ago?"

"Yeah...?"

"And what did you tell me?"

Ryan hesitated for a minute and finally agreed that a night out might do her some good.

The next day at the gym, Brandon greeted me with a kiss as I came out of the locker room. We worked out together like we had on Monday. I told him my plans for the evening and he mentioned that he and Jason played poker with some of their buddies on Wednesdays. After our workout, I grabbed my stuff from the locker room and he offered to give me a ride home. Since I used public transportation to get to work, I didn't mind getting a ride home from the gym.

As we pulled up to my house, Brandon kissed me goodnight and made sure I was going to be at the gym on

Thursday. Assuring him that I would be, I blew him a kiss and waved before turning to go inside.

Ryan was already getting ready for our night out and seemed to be in a good mood. I quickly got ready and we made our way to Fog City Diner. We sat in one of the black leather booths by the window and ordered the "Mac & Cheese", three chicken tacos to split and Cosmopolitans. Fog City Diner was famous for being in the movie *So I Married an Axe Murder* and was always packed with customers. It was an upscale fifties diner with black and white checkerboard patterns throughout.

Shortly after our food arrived, I glanced up at the door and saw Max walking in with a girl. She had dark brown hair and was wearing jeans and a grey and white striped sweater. I was so thankful that Ryan's back was to the door. Then Max noticed me and I gave him the look of death––the look that spoke volumes. *If you come over here and fuck with Ryan, I will so fuck your shit up!*

Max leaned over and whispered something into the girl's ear. They both looked at me and smiled and then they left, not looking back behind them. Thankfully they were not holding hands or I might have chased Max down and kicked his ass.

"What's wrong?" Ryan asked while I let out the breath I didn't realize I was holding in.

"Oh... nothing. I thought I saw Travis." There was no way in hell I was going to tell her who I really saw.

"I better not see that piece of shit or I will fuck him up for you, Spence!" Yep, we were definitely best friends, two peas in a pod and I loved her!

After dinner, Ryan and I took a cab over to The Mint, which was packed by the time we arrived. Over the course of the night, Ryan and I got extremely tipsy and sang very badly. I didn't care because all I wanted was for Ryan to have fun and we were having a great time.

The next morning I woke up with a splitting headache. I didn't remember coming home last night but I was dressed in my PJs and alone in my bed. I quickly got in the shower, got dressed for work and made my way out to the kitchen for my morning coffee.

Glancing at my phone to see what time it was, I noticed I had a missed text from Brandon:

Brandon: *Yes, night baby!*

Holy shit. Baby? Did I miss something? I didn't remember texting Brandon last night! Panic ran through me and I quickly scrolled up...

10:49 p.m.

Me: *Hi, I miss u!*

Brandon: *I miss you too Spence. Are you and Ryan having fun?*

Me: *Yes, Ryan is doing Karaoke right now singing Party in the USA!*

Brandon: *I wish I could see that, lol.*

11:11 p.m.

Me: *I wish u were here! I would soooooo go down on u in the bathroom.*

Brandon: *While that sounds tempting, the guys would never let me live it down if I ditched them for a chick right now.*

71

Me: *What if it was TWO hot chicks going down on you?*

Two hot chicks? Oh my God, I would never! I kept saying Oh my God as I continued reading...

Brandon: *LOL, how many drinks have you had?*

11:16 p.m.

Me: *Um... I have only had like 5 vodka cranberries.*

Brandon: *Well then I would say you're drunk. Be safe ok?*

11:20 p.m.

Brandon: *Spence, are you ok?*

11:22 p.m.

Brandon: *Hello?*

11:29 p.m.

Me: *Sorry, Ryan and I sang a duet. We are being safe. Come see me, NOW!!!*

Brandon: *I wish I could but like I said, the boys would give me shit.*

Me: *Fine I see how it is! :)*

Brandon: *Don't be like that baby. I would if I could!*

11:59 p.m.

Me: *Ryan and I just got home. I'm going to sleep with B.O.B. now... Night!*

Brandon: *Baby, you're killing me. I'm going to have to confiscate that thing from you.*

Me: *I would rather DO the real thing!*

Brandon: *Tomorrow, I promise.*

Me: *Really?*

Brandon: *Yes, night baby.*

Oh. My. God. Did I just plan to have sex with Brandon...tonight? Two chicks? Going down on him in the bathroom? What the fuck did I do? How am I ever going to face him again? Ah I didn't even shave my legs this morning!

I wasn't feeling well but I still made it to work on time. I could tell this day was going to be hell since I had a hangover. Around ten o'clock, Brandon texted to ask me how I was feeling. I stared at the text for the longest time. I had no idea what to say to him. Was he expecting to get laid tonight? I know we had some hot moments together, but I couldn't believe that I had actually "scheduled" it for tonight.

Brandon: *Hey, how are you feeling today?*

Me: *My head feels like it got hit with a sledge hammer.*

Brandon: *Too much alcohol will do that to you. Will I still see you later at the gym?*

Oh God, here it was. He was expecting me to follow through with my text.

Me: *Yes, of course.*

Brandon: *What are you doing after the gym?*

Was he expecting me to say "you"? I wanted to say "you"! He was starting to become like a drug. I thought about him constantly and just wanted to be around him.

Me: *Yeah about that...I don't remember texting you last night...*

Brandon: *I figured you wouldn't. I knew you were drunk texting. But I have to admit that I do hope in the future we can do what you said. :)*

Relief washed over me, then was quickly followed by panic. Did he mean the two girl thing or the blowjob in the bathroom? Oh God!

Me: *Yeah about that too... I have never been with another girl.*

Brandon: *You're so cute. That's not what I meant. Anyway, I'll see you after work.*

Me: *K :)*

I finally started to feel better after lunch; thankfully the afternoon went faster than the morning. I arrived at the gym to what I hoped would continue to be my daily greeting: a kiss from Brandon. "How are you feeling? Do you really want to work out today?"

He obviously could see right through me. I really didn't want to work out and had only come because I had promised I would and really wanted to see him.

"I am feeling better but I really don't want to work out."

"Good, I have other plans."

Aw shit, was it time? I knew I should have shaved my legs at lunch!

He took me by the hand and escorted me to the spa at the gym. The spa? What the...

"Every week I get a massage. This week it happens to be today," Brandon said with the smirk I loved to see so much.

"What? Really?"

"Perks of owning the place."

I'd say. I would love to get a massage every week! We walked up to the front desk and we were greeted by a cute brunette named Ari who blushed immediately when we approached the desk.

"Ari, Ms. Marshall will be joining me this evening."

"Of course, Mr. Montgomery."

We were handed robes and he escorted me to the women's locker room. He said he would meet me at the exit door inside the locker room. Inside the locker room I noticed that they had all the amenities: combs, shampoo, conditioner, lotion, body wash and a razor. *A razor! Score.* I hurried to shave my legs and then made my way out to meet Brandon.

We were brought into the couple's room where Brandon thankfully let me get under the sheet on the table before entering the room. For some reason I was still a bit shy and embarrassed. When he came in, I slyly caught a glimpse of his rock hard ass. I just wanted to reach out and squeeze it!

I didn't realize how tense my body was until Christa, my massage therapist, started to rub out the kinks. The scent of the eucalyptus oil she used was soothing and refreshing and I was almost asleep on the table when Christa whispered in my ear that our session was over. I slowly opened my eyes and looked over at Brandon as he looked back at me and gave me that smile. I had to admit that the massage had been amazing; a girl could really get used to this sort of treatment.

CHAPTER SIX

Brandon picked me up at 5:30 p.m. on Friday for the Giants game. The game didn't start until 7:15 p.m., but he and Jason had a ritual of going early to drink beers and get food before the game. After our massages the night before, he had driven me home and kissed me goodnight again. Disappointment hit, but I was also thankful that he knew I had been drunk texting the night before. Liquid courage always made me brave.

He drove us to his condo which wasn't far from AT&T Park. We walked the few blocks and greeted Jason and Becca, who were waiting for us outside the gates.

"It's so good to see you again, Spencer," Becca said as she greeted me with a warm hug that I thought was strange but also nice. It had been almost a week since Vegas when I had seen them last.

We made our way to get beer, hot dogs, nachos and the famous *Gilroy Garlic Fries* that they served at the park. After grabbing our food, we headed over to our seats which were on the third base line in the lower box. To my surprise, Becca made her way down the row first, followed by me, Brandon and then Jason.

"We can chat when the game gets boring," Becca said as she noticed my face. "I see Jason every day!"

We ate our food and drank our beers while watching batting practice for the *San Diego Padres*. Over the course of the night, Becca and I got to know each other better and I could really see her becoming a friend. I learned that she was a photographer and had an upcoming show at a local gallery in a few weeks, which she invited me and Ryan to attend.

Before the game they held a little ceremony during which Buster Posey was presented with the *Willie Mac Award*. Some of the previous winners were in attendance as well as Willie Mac himself.

During the game, Brandon continually rested his hand on my knee. At first it gave me butterflies, but after a while my pulse rate returned to normal. Most fans were dressed in their orange Giants jerseys or shirts. Luckily I remembered that Fridays were Orange Friday for the Giants and had worn my Giants shirt in that color.

The game was very exciting. Crawford, Posey and Scutaro all hit RBIs and the Panda hit a two-run homer in the bottom of the sixth. We sang the traditional seventh inning stretch song in the middle of the seventh, and in the middle of the eighth, the whole stadium sang Journey's song *Lights*.

I was having an amazing time. The Giants won seven to one and I was getting to see another side of Brandon as I watched him react to each play. He and Jason yelled at the top of their lungs and gestured wildly several times through the night. When Panda hit his two-run homer in the bottom of the sixth, they turned to each other and whooped before bumping chests and roaring. Becca and I exchanged glances at that, rolling our eyes and laughing. Boys! After the game, Brandon and I walked back to his two-story condo that overlooked China Basin.

While he grabbed us beers from the fridge, I took a look around his condo. The downstairs had an open floor plan with floor-to-ceiling windows and dark hardwood floors. As you continued from the living room into the kitchen, there were cherry wood cabinets with black granite countertops and stainless steel appliances.

He had dark brown leather couches surrounding a cherry wood coffee table that sat on a beige rug, matching end tables and a huge flat screen TV mounted over the fireplace. It reminded me of a bachelor pad minus the *Ikea* brand furniture.

Next to the breakfast bar which was between the kitchen and living room hung a black and white picture of The Golden Gate Bridge on a foggy day. "That's one of Becca's," Brandon said when he noticed me looking at it.

"Wow, it is beautiful!"

"She invited you to her show on the twenty-eighth, right?" I nodded. "Care to be my date for the night?"

"Sure, sounds like fun. Oh and Becca said that Ryan should come as well. Mind if she tags along?" Given Ryan's new single status, I knew another night out would be good for her.

"No, of course not." Within seconds, Brandon was right in front of me. He grabbed my beer and set it on the counter, cupping the right side of my face as he slid his fingers through my hair and kissed me. His tongue extended further into my mouth as he deepened the kiss. I wrapped my arms around his neck to steady myself as my knees began to weaken.

"I've wanted to do that all night!" he said as he broke free from our kiss. He took my hand and led me to his couch. "I'm not ready for you to go home, yet––want to watch a movie?"

"Sure," I agreed, while I sat down on the couch.

Brandon turned on the TV while he sat down next to me. "Do you like action, comedy, horror...?"

"Action or comedy is fine." He chose *Mission Impossible: Ghost Protocol.* I had already seen the movie but really didn't care. I wasn't ready to go home either and I didn't plan on watching the movie anyway. I quickly grabbed my phone to text Ryan:

Me: *Going to watch a movie at Brandon's, might not be home. Don't wait up! :)*

As the movie started I nuzzled myself into Brandon's left side. He placed his left arm around my shoulders while getting comfortable. Not long after the movie started, he leaned over and lifted my chin to give me another kiss. I sat up and faced him allowing him to kiss me better. He slowly leaned me back on the couch while running kisses along my neck. His left knee was wedged between my legs and his other leg stood balancing on the floor.

Caressing my back with one hand, he lifted the hem of my shirt enough to reach under and caress my left breast. A moan escaped my mouth as he returned to kiss my lips, then broke away to nuzzle a trail of kisses down my neck and back up to my ear. My toes curled in delight as his teeth and tongue did dangerous things to my earlobe. I slid my hands down his back feeling his muscular shoulders and back.

Out of the corner of my eye I saw an incoming call light up on Brandon's phone as it lay on a nearby coffee table. I didn't want to stop and he didn't seem to notice. I started to tug on his shirt to pull it over his head. Electricity was running through my body as he lifted my shirt higher, released my left breast from the cup of my bra and began sucking on my already hard nipple.

He pulled my shirt over my head and then stripped his off as well, tossing one after the other on the floor. My breasts became heavy; my clit throbbed, wanting attention while my legs slid apart allowing him to lower his hips against mine. He turned his attention to my right breast, teasing my nipple with his tongue. "Put your legs around my waist," Brandon said as he flicked my nipple once more with his tongue.

Confused, I did as I was told as he scooped me up with one hand behind my back and began to stand. My arms wrapped around his neck and I continued to kiss him. He began walking up the stairs with me wrapped around his hips.

When we reached the top of the stairs, he continued walking into a room that I assumed was his bedroom. He laid me down on the foot of the bed, running his fingers down my belly and began to unbutton my jeans.

At his urging, I lifted my hips off the bed, allowing my jeans to be tugged off my legs. He hooked his fingers inside my panties, taking them as well. I was left only in my bra. While gazing at my openness Brandon licked his lips, triggering a growing tightness deep in my belly.

Kneeling, he spread my legs wider and began to kiss slowly down my right inner thigh, letting his lips slide across the sensitive skin of one leg and then switching to the other. Finally, he moved up and hovered above the apex of my thighs and just breathed above me. I was dying from the anticipation and groaned as I arched my hips up, desperate to feel his mouth on me. I felt bumps rise rapidly on my skin and I gasped loudly, which quickly turned into a deep and satisfied moan as his tongue sought out the lips of my pussy. This was what I had been waiting for all my life – this was the way it was supposed to feel.

I spread my legs wider and arched my hips higher, urging him to lick deeper. Using two fingers, he gently spread my lips and licked the sides of my pussy and the nub of my clit. Pleasure pulsed through me as my body heat rose. He slid one long finger into me while he continued to suck and lick like he couldn't get enough. Panting, I let out another moan when he slid another finger into me. My pussy clenched tightly around him as I closed my eyes, enjoying his skilled fingers and tongue.

My hands ran through his hair as he continued licking while sliding his fingers in and out of me. I could feel the tension building; I was on the brink of climaxing and feeling as if I would combust at any second. Brandon started rubbing my clit with his thumb as he continued using his fingers. I found my release as I let out a cry, my body sending vibrations through me as I climaxed around his fingers.

Pulling away, Brandon stripped off his pants and boxers at the same time. I removed my bra and tossed it on the floor. God he was gorgeous in all his glory: broad shoulders, chiseled chest, six-pack abs that were attached to a sexy v-cut that lead all the way down to his impressive cock.

He crawled on top of me to lead me back further on the bed. Leaning over, he kissed my lips and slowly slid his tongue into my mouth. I could taste myself on him and warmth ran through me, straight to my sweet spot.

His right arm wrapped around my back as I arched into his chest, flesh on flesh. He slowly caressed his hand down my back, squeezing my ass into his hand. I could feel his erection throbbing against my bare thigh.

I moved my hands to cup his face and lightly bit his lower lip. "Biting me again, Spence?" Brandon said while he leaned up and reached over to the drawer of the nightstand to pull out a condom. Ripping the package with his teeth, he removed the condom and rolled it expertly onto his shaft.

He adjusted my legs to spread them farther apart. I could smell my arousal as his erection touched the entrance of my pussy that was dripping with the need for him to be thrusting inside me. He moved slowly at first, drawing out each stroke, almost pulling out of me completely, but then pushing deeply back into me. Finally he began to thrust faster, his cock growing even stiffer as he pumped harder and harder, over and over. Running my fingers through his soft hair, I returned my lips to his. My tongue explored his mouth again, tasting the remainder of my juices.

His thrusts increased with speed again and another moan escaped my mouth. He kissed me hard as his teeth tugged at my lower lip. I could feel my orgasm building as he dug his hips deep into me. My body started to quiver as his breath increased. Continuing to thrust harder and harder he came right after my body found its release for the second time.

"Shower with me?" Brandon said as he kissed me once more.

CHAPTER SEVEN

If someone would have told me a week ago that I would be waking up to kisses on my neck from Brandon this morning, I would have thought they were crazy. After our um..."shower" last night, he gave me one of his t-shirts to wear and asked me if I wanted to stay the night. I was living in a dream and waking up like this was one of the best feelings in the world.

"Mornin' beautiful," Brandon said when he saw I was waking up.

"Morning," I replied and turned over to kiss him on the lips and snuggle closer into him.

"What would you like to do today?"

"You", I wanted to say, but I chickened out. "I don't care; I'm up for anything as long as I can run home and get clean clothes." I was scared that at any moment I would wake up from this dream and be on my couch in my pajamas with a bowl of melted mint chocolate chip ice cream on the coffee table.

"Okay, get dressed while I go downstairs and make us breakfast. Then we will swing by your place." He kissed me once more, then left to go downstairs. I stayed in bed for a little while longer remembering the night before and pinched myself to make sure this was really happening.

The dark cherry hardwood floors from the first floor continued to the second. His bed sat in the middle of the bedroom with a low wall behind the headboard. Behind the wall were floor-to-ceiling windows along the whole room and glass doors that led to a balcony overlooking the China Basin.

His bed sat on a chocolate brown wood platform that was low to the ground. The mattress didn't cover the whole platform, allowing a step on each side of the mattress and the foot of the bed. His sheets were white and brown striped with matching pillows and the comforter was solid milk chocolate brown with a large square pattern embroidered on it. He had the traditional nightstands and dressers that matched the bedroom set.

A cream rug sat under the bed separating the browns from each other. The masculine room décor was completed with a large flat screen TV that hung over a fireplace on the far wall. Clearly no woman had ever lived here.

After reminiscing, I got up and got dressed making my way downstairs. The smell of bacon filled my nostrils and I heard Brandon talking when I reached the top of the stairs. I stopped walking, not wanting to interrupt his conversation.

"I told you to stop calling me; this isn't a good time... No, I don't care – I can't talk to you right now. I'm not doing this anymore with you.... I told you I was done... No, just stop calling me please... it's over and I have nothing more to say to you." Then I heard the phone drop into its cradle.

I waited a few more seconds before I finished walking down the stairs. When I got to the bottom, I headed to the kitchen where I found Brandon making scrambled eggs, with bacon cooking in the oven.

"Yum, it smells so good in here," I said as I walked over to where my shirt was lying on the floor. After putting it back on, I walked over to where Brandon was cooking and wrapped my arms around his waist from behind while placing my head on his back and hugged him. He didn't know I heard his phone conversation, so he didn't mention anything about the call to me. I figured it was his ex Christy calling and I knew how hard break-ups are, so I didn't mention it either.

～

After breakfast we made our way to my place so I could change into clean clothes. Ryan was lying on the couch still in her pajamas when we walked in.

"Hey Ry, whatcha doin'?" I asked.

"You know, lying around feeding my face." My heart broke for her. I was the same way only a few weeks ago.

"Come on, why don't you come to the zoo with us?" I glanced over to Brandon and gave him a questioning glance and a smile. He nodded in confirmation.

"I don't want to be a third wheel."

"You're not. Please come, it'll be fun."

Ryan still seemed reluctant, but she finally caved and agreed to come.

"Good, now I'm going to jump in the shower real quick and when I am done, you can shower and get ready. We'll wait for you," I said as I started to walk to my room.

Brandon sat down on the opposite couch that we had in the living room and started watching *HGTV* with Ryan. I quickly hurried and took a shower. Dressing in my robe, I walked to my room and yelled to Ryan that the shower was free.

When I entered my room Brandon was waiting for me. He didn't say a word as he walked over and closed the door behind me.

"What's wrong?" I asked, but he still didn't say a word.

He backed me up so my back was against the door. His hands were on both sides of my head, pinning me where I stood. "Wha…" Before I could ask him again what was wrong, his lips were on mine, parting them and exploring my mouth with his tongue. He started to untie my robe. "Wait, Ryan is here and she might hear us," I said, breaking our kiss.

"She'll be in the shower," Brandon said, and returned to kiss me and finished untying my robe.

He slipped my robe over my shoulders and it puddled onto the floor around my feet. I was completely naked and at his mercy. His hands palmed my ass and pulled me in hard against his jeans, letting me feel his erection. I lifted his shirt and pulled it over his head, dropping it on the floor with my robe.

My eyes drifted to his chest. "You have a tattoo...I didn't see this last night."

It had been dark last night and my eyes had been closed most of the time as I enjoyed his touch; then during our shower...he was behind me.

His tattoo was on the upper right side of his abs. While tracing my fingers over the script I read it to myself: *Pain is inevitable. Suffering is optional.*

"I'll tell you about it when we have more time," he said as he kneaded my right breast with his hand and lifted it enough so his tongue could swirl around my nipple. My clit began to throb while I felt moisture building between my legs.

Releasing my breast, he slipped his hand between my legs and thrust two fingers deep inside while his thumb circled my clit. I broke our kiss to scream out in ecstasy but Brandon placed his hand over my mouth before I could let out a peep.

"Shhhh, Ryan might hear," he said.

I unbuttoned his pants and pushed them down with his boxers enough to release him. Wrapping my hand around his length I began stroking his erection. I felt a drop of pre-cum on the tip of his cock as I continued to stroke his hard smooth shaft while his fingers plunged deeper inside me.

Brandon removed his fingers as he reached into the pocket of his jeans and pulled out a condom. Ripping the foil open with his teeth, he rolled the condom onto his cock. Then he lifted me up so my legs wrapped around him and slowly entered inch by inch. I buried my face in his neck and bit my bottom lip as pleasure shot through my entire body.

My lower back slid up and down against the door as he thrust deep inside me. He cupped my ass to spread me a little wider to allow himself to go deeper. All too soon, I felt my body begin to quiver.

With a few more thrusts my body began to shatter into a million pieces. I buried my face deeper into his neck trying to stop myself from crying out. He stilled as he found his own release while bracing himself on the door with his left hand.

With our bodies still joined, he cupped my cheeks and placed his lips on mine once more. He gently lowered me to the ground and kissed the top of my head. Removing the condom, he tied the end and placed it in a tissue before tossing it in the small trash can I had near my desk. He began to pull up his pants as I grabbed a pair of panties from my dresser.

"So *HGTV* turns you on?" I said, smirking at him.

"No, you naked in the other room turns me on!" he replied as he swatted my butt playfully.

We dressed and then Brandon sat on my queen size bed as he glanced around. "I like your room and especially your *bed*," he said, stretching himself out on my bed set which was complete with latte colored sheets and a beige comforter with large sea green and brown chrysanthemums.

"Thanks," I grinned. While I did my make-up and finished getting ready, he checked some emails on his phone and made a quick phone call to Jason. When we exited my room, Ryan was still in her room getting ready. When she was finally ready, we made our way to the zoo. It was a gorgeous day and perfect to spend outdoors.

After our day at the zoo, we drove back to my house so that Ryan and I could change for dinner. Brandon said that he really enjoyed Ryan's company and we all decided to go out to dinner. It made me happy that we were all getting along and Ryan wouldn't be spending a Saturday night alone. I think Brandon had the same idea.

After Ryan and I changed, we drove to Brandon's place so he could change. With a hushed voice Ryan whispered, "Damn Spence, his place is really nice!"

I agreed with her. I was feeling lucky; I couldn't believe what had happened in only a few weeks.

"You girls ready?" Brandon said as he walked down the stairs.

We walked a few blocks to MoMo's which was located across from AT&T Park. The Giants game was in progress across the street and on the TVs at MoMo's. We found a three top table that was located near the bar so we could watch the game.

Towards the end of dinner, the bar started to fill up as the Giants game ended. They had clinched the Western Division Conference and everyone was going crazy with excitement.

As the bar started to meet capacity, I noticed Travis walk in with Misty. *Great!* Under the table I squeezed Ryan's leg to get her attention.

"What?" she asked, leaning over so only I could hear her.

I whispered in her ear, "Travis just walked in".

"What? Where?" *So much for being quiet about it!*

"Where's what?" Brandon asked, joining the conversation. *Just fucking great.*

"Spencer's ex just walked in," Ryan said, informing Brandon of our private conversation.

All three of us were now staring at the door that Travis and Misty walked through. They walked over to the bar and started talking to people I didn't know.

"I'm going to go over there and give him a piece of my mind!" Ryan said as she started to stand up.

Tugging on her arm so she couldn't move, I said, "Oh no you don't, I don't want anything to do with him anymore."

Before I realized it, Brandon was already walking over to Travis. "Holy shit, what is he doing?" I asked Ryan in a panic.

"Looks like he is going to go over and talk to Travis."

"He can't talk to Travis! Why does he want to talk to Travis?" I felt totally panicked and I couldn't have moved an inch if my life depended on it. I was frozen to my seat as I watched Brandon approach Travis.

We sat there stunned as we watched the silent movie play in front of us. My heart was pounding in my chest and my palms became sweaty. In the few seconds it took Brandon to reach Travis, a million scenarios ran through my head. Then Brandon said something to Travis making him and Misty look over at us. Misty rolled her eyes at me and Brandon reached out and shook Travis' hand. Travis looked pissed as he glanced first at me and then at Brandon and then back at me again.

Brandon started walking back to our table smiling and Travis returned to staring at me. If looks could kill, I would be dead by the evil glare of Misty.

When Brandon reached our table he planted a kiss on my lips. "What did you say to him?" I asked as I looked over at Travis and Misty, who were still staring.

"I just told him thank you for being a douche bag and giving me the opportunity to treat you the way you are supposed to be treated."

My heart melted. I leaned over and kissed Brandon again. Leaning my face back a little I whispered, "thank you," and kissed his lips again.

"Ah you guys are so cute, but you're making me jealous over here!" Ryan said with a huff.

CHAPTER EIGHT

After dinner, we went back to Brandon's place so he could get his car and take us home. Once we were home, Brandon walked us to the door.

"Stay with me tonight?" I asked. He nodded and I grabbed his hand leading him to my room.

"Night guys," Ryan said as she went to her room.

Quietly, I closed the door behind us. Without saying a word, I pushed Brandon on the bed so he fell on his back.

"What are you doing?" he said as he gave me a sly look.

"Shh, let me show you how thankful I am for what you did tonight."

I unbuttoned his pants and pulled them off while tossing them and his boxers on the floor. His legs dangled over the edge of my bed as I knelt down in front of him. I gripped his length with the palm of my right hand and swirled my wet tongue around the head of his cock.

While I ran my tongue along each side of his cock, he let out a moan. His hands grabbed fistfuls of my hair urging me on. I took his cock in my mouth, sucking him deep. I sucked harder while pulling back and running my tongue along the tip again, tasting his salty pre-cum.

With my mouth still on his cock, I ran my left hand under his shirt and over his smooth skin and perfect abs while my right hand cupped his balls.

"Fuck baby," he whispered.

Massaging his balls with my hand, I gently drew his cock in and out of my mouth over and over. Swirling my tongue around his tip, I began to lick his salty pre-cum. I pushed him deeper into the back of my throat while I slowly fucked him with my mouth.

Releasing my hand from his balls, I held the base of his cock firmly and continued to suck him deep. He groaned again with pleasure. While bobbing my head up and down, faster and faster, his hands tightened their grip in my hair.

"Baby, I'm going to come," he said in warning.

I continued sucking his cock as he tensed and then groaned loudly as he spurted hot cum down the back of my throat. After the last drop, I released his cock from my mouth and licked it once more.

Brandon and I rose as he reached out to grab my shirt and pulled it over my head. While he was unbuttoning my jeans, I took my bra off and tossed it on the floor. I began to step out of my jeans while he took his shirt off. He laced his fingers in the inside of my panties and tugged them down and tossed them into the pile of clothes.

He sat back down on the edge of the bed and reached out and drew my body against his as he placed kisses on my belly. Cupping my right breast, he flicked my nipple making it hard. He shifted his focus to my left breast that was aching for attention and repeated what he had done on my right.

I ran my hands through his hair as I closed my eyes. He scooted back on my bed as I followed crawling on top of him. To my surprise, Brandon kissed me as his tongue swirled in my mouth. TravAss would never kiss me after I went down on him – not until I had brushed my teeth.

Brandon continued to kiss me, deeply and passionately. I felt his hand reach between my legs and he began circling my nub. He rolled me onto the bed with my back against the mattress and continued teasing me with his thumb.

He wrapped his hands behind each of my legs and scooted down so his face was between them. He ran light kisses along the inside of my thighs until his mouth found my pussy. He stroked my clit with the tip of his tongue and then sucked it into his mouth.

My legs started to clench together and I groaned. Brandon continued sucking and licking my clit until I reached my climax. My thighs quivered as the delicious sensations ran through my body.

Brandon rose onto his knees. "There's a condom in the drawer of my nightstand," I said as I was coming down from my high.

After he put the condom on, he traced the entrance of my pussy with the tip of his erection. I shifted my hips to allow him to enter as he settled between my thighs sliding into me with one smooth motion. His thrusts were slow and deep as he filled me. He placed both of my hands above my head as he ran his tongue down over each breast. Arching my back in response, I groaned again.

His tongue ran up my body as he sought out my lips. His lips tasted and smelled like me. He released my hands and I moved them to his ass and pulled him harder and deeper into me as my legs wrapped around his waist taking him all in. I could feel the faint moisture of sweat on his body. "Roll over," I whispered to let him know I wanted to be on top.

He slid out of me and turned over on his back. I straddled his hips and sank down onto his cock, taking him deep inside me again. My head tilted back as his hands grazed my breasts.

I bent down and kissed his tattoo that I had discovered earlier in the day. I slid my hips back and forth against his cock. His hand found my clit and he stroked it as my hips continued to glide back and forth.

He moved his hips to meet mine, stroke after stroke. My eyes closed as he pumped into me. We rocked back and forth as his thumb continued to circle my clit. My body reached its climax as sensation rippled through it. Brandon shuddered as he thrust one last time into me.

❧

The next morning I woke to Brandon's body pressed into mine from behind and his arms were wrapped tightly around me. Trying not to wake him, I inched out of bed and made my way to the kitchen to start coffee and breakfast.

Ryan joined me as I put the bacon in the oven. "Whatcha makin'?"

"Bacon, eggs, potatoes...you know, breakfast."

"Is Brandon still here?"

"Yeah, and he's still sleeping, so keep it down."

Whispering she said, "What do you think of him approaching Trav*Ass* last night?"

"Dude, I thought I was going to pass out or die of embarrassment. But when he came back and told me what he said, I wanted to jump and smother him with kisses," I said, whispering as well.

"I wanted to do the same thing!"

"Ha...well he's mine!"

"I'm so happy for you, Spence... and really jealous."

"You'll find someone, Ry. I promise."

I continued to cook breakfast, hoping Brandon wouldn't wake up before I could surprise him in bed. Right before everything was ready, Brandon walked into the kitchen.

"Morning, ladies," he said as he walked over, kissed my cheek and hugged me from behind. "That smells really good!"

"It's bacon, nothing smells as good as bacon!" I said, smiling as I continued to cook the scrambled eggs.

"Hey, Spence, what are we doing for your birthday?" Ryan asked.

"What? When is your birthday?" Brandon asked in surprise.

Somehow I had failed to mention to Brandon that my birthday was in less than a week.

"Um, this coming Saturday."

"You weren't going to tell me?" Brandon asked with hurt in his voice.

"No, not at all. It just completely slipped my mind!" It really had. I'd had a lot to keep my mind occupied as of late.

Usually every year I was excited about my birthday, but after this last week with Brandon, I'm surprised I even knew what day it was.

"So what are we doing?" Ryan asked again.

"I don't know but I'm open to suggestions. Let's discuss while we eat so the food doesn't get cold."

During breakfast we decided that for my birthday we would take a day trip to the Santa Cruz Beach Boardwalk. It seemed the older you became, the more you just wanted to do kid things for your birthday. A day filled with roller coasters, fried food and cotton candy sounded perfect to me.

Brandon stayed over at my house all day and we spent the majority of it lounging in bed while we watched TV. Okay, in all honesty, not a lot of TV was actually watched. And I didn't even get dressed for the day. I couldn't remember the last time I had felt this happy.

"Will you tell me about your tattoo?" I asked Brandon during a commercial as we lounged naked in my bed.

"Oh, yeah...sure." Brandon let out a long sigh then took a deep breath. I immediately regretted asking him when I saw how sad and serious he became.

"Remember how I told you the other night at dinner that during my sophomore year at *Texas A&M* I got hurt and never played again?"

"Yeah...?"

"The guy who I was competing against for starting quarterback had it out for me. He was a senior and assumed he would be starting, but then our coach told the team that it would be me instead. That night Jason and I went to a party on campus and we were jumped by six guys... Actually, I should say *I* was jumped by six guys. They all attacked me while Jason tried to pull them off of me. In the midst of everything, they managed to break my back."

"Oh my God!" I gasped, my heart breaking for him. I couldn't imagine going through that – couldn't imagine the pain he must have endured.

"Thankfully, there was no damage to my spinal cord and to make a long story short, I had to do a lot of physical therapy until I was able to walk again. It was later found out that the guys who jumped me were all fraternity brothers of my teammate. He was expelled, but since I was out of commission, they had to find a replacement. Then in my junior year I still couldn't play, so I ended up never playing again... So... my tattoo just reminds me that no matter what challenges I may face, I will get through anything life throws my way. *Pain is inevitable. Suffering is optional* has become my motto, and Jason and I are very successful and already looking to expand again."

"Do you know what happened to the guy?"

"Nope, I haven't seen him since the day his mommy and daddy came to collect him from school." Brandon laughed when he said "mommy and daddy"; it made me feel a little better about his story.

"That is really sad. I am sorry you had to go through that!"

"It's okay. It's made me stronger and if none of that had happened, I might not have ever met you." Brandon leaned down to kiss me.

It was getting late in the evening and all I wanted was to stay in Brandon's arms until Monday morning. I didn't care that I had a ton of laundry to do. I could put everything on hold just to stay right where I was.

"Babe?" *Did Brandon just call me "Babe"?* This was the first time he had said it in person. The only other time was when I was drunk texting. I got butterflies in my stomach just for the one simple word.

"Yeah?" I answered, my head resting on his chest.

"Do you want to stay at my place tonight or here? If you want to stay here, then I need to run home and pack an overnight bag." He wanted to stay the night with me again? Of course I wanted to stay with him, but I didn't want to seem too eager or clingy. After all, it hadn't even been a week.

"I don't care. Whatever you want to do is fine with me."

"Well, since I would have to go home anyway, why don't we just stay there?"

"Ok, that sounds good."

"I'll even drive you to work in the morning," he offered. Like I really needed an incentive?

"Well, twist my arm why don't you."

And just like that Brandon pinned my hands under me...

CHAPTER NINE

It was the third morning in a row that I had woken up in Brandon's arms. Each time I prayed to myself that this was real. I was starting to fall hard for him. In just a week he had made me feel like I was the only person in the world. I was pretty sure I was falling in love with him.

Brandon drove me to work as he promised and kissed me thoroughly before I got out of the car. As I walked into the office humming to myself with a silly grin plastered on my face, I thought to myself that I could definitely get used to this. After work, I met him at the gym and we worked out together like we had the previous week. Then we went back to my place and I cooked spaghetti and meatballs for both us and Ryan. Brandon surprised me by lending a hand and making the best garlic bread I had ever tasted and Ryan contributed a tiramisu she had picked up on her way home from work.

After dinner, we all lounged around in the living room watching *The Voice*. Ryan seemed to be over her depression of Max. However, she was still hanging out around the house a lot when she wasn't at work. I felt bad for flaunting my relationship in front of her, but I was thankful that all three of us were getting along really well.

To my delight Brandon spent the night again, but the next morning, I woke to an empty bed. An initial feeling of disappointment ran through me until I saw his shirt hanging on my desk chair. I walked out of my room and saw Ryan in the kitchen drinking her coffee.

"Mornin'!," she said brightly as I yawned sleepily, rubbing my tired eyes. She was always a morning person, but I usually needed some caffeine before I started to feel human again. Turning to the cabinet, she rummaged for another mug and then poured some coffee. "Here, you look like you need this."

"Gee thanks." I stuck my tongue out at her, but gratefully accepted the steaming mug. "Have you seen Brandon?"

"Oh yeah, I think he's in the shower right now."

Oh really? This could be interesting.

I hurried back to my room, trying not to spill my hot coffee along the way. Setting it down on my dresser, I grabbed a paperclip to stick in the tiny hole of the bathroom doorknob. Our house was older and we had never replaced the old doorknobs, which was extremely convenient for me at the moment.

I quietly popped the lock and opened the door. Removing my PJs, I dropped them in a pile on the floor and slowly opened the foggy glass door of the wall length tile shower trying not to make a sound. Trying not to giggle, I slipped in the back of the shower. At that moment Brandon was facing me with his eyes closed and head tilted back as he rinsed the shampoo from his hair.

When he finished, his head straightened and he smiled slowly as he noticed me standing there.

"Hey baby," he said when our eyes locked. "What a nice surprise."

"Hey," I said as I slipped my arms around his neck kissing him. "Too bad we don't have enough time to take advantage of us both being in the shower together."

He pulled me closer against his dripping wet, naked body and I felt him begin to harden against my belly. "Yes, that is a shame. Maybe we should set your alarm thirty minutes earlier?"

"Maybe..." Of course, I wasn't a morning person, but if it involved showering with Brandon every morning, I could make an exception.

～∽

Brandon and I went to the Tuesday kickboxing class after work. We arrived to the class early and started to stretch a little as we waited for the instructor to arrive and start class.

"Oh, Brandon, there you are."

Brandon and I turned around when I heard a lady address him. When I fully turned, I noticed she was an older lady in what I guessed to be her late fifties with long blond highlighted hair, dark blue eyes, a small mole on the left side of her face under her lip and obviously fake boobs. I got the impression she had money for some reason.

"Oh, hello, Mrs. Robinson, how are you this evening?"

"Brandon, you know I am not married and please call me Teresa." Teresa took that opportunity to step closer to Brandon and rub her hand down his left arm taking extra time on his bicep. *Mrs. Robinson? Well this was ironic.* "I wanted to ask you when you would give me that private lesson we talked about."

Brandon stepped back away from Teresa and moved closer to me. "Teresa, remember we talked about you having a private session with one of my best personal trainers I have on staff?"

"I remember, honey, I just want *you* to do it." Teresa's eyes darted to her right in my direction and sized me up. I took that opportunity to grab *my* man's left hand, clearly showing her I was more than a friend and workout buddy. Brandon squeezed my hand in response.

"Teresa, you know I don't do personal trainings anymore and only work in the office, which is why we talked about getting one of my best trainers for you."

"Won't you make an exception?" Wow, I didn't know "older" women would stoop that low and beg with puppy dog eyes and a quivering bottom lip, but sure enough Teresa was doing it. "I would be interested in more than one private session which I would pay handsomely for."

"Teresa, we can talk about this tomorrow if you'd like to come by my office before five o'clock. I can show you the binder of trainers we offer. I just don't have the time right now with us expanding in Seattle, but I do value your business and will have you choose from only my best trainers." *Seattle? I didn't know they were expanding.*

"If you insist, I will see *you* tomorrow." Teresa gave me a half-hearted smile and winked at Brandon, then walked away to the front of the class as the instructor started the music to begin class.

~

After our kickboxing class, Brandon and I went to dinner at The Slanted Door.

"Oh babe, before I forget, Thursday morning Jason and I are flying to Seattle and won't be back until Friday afternoon, but we'll be back in time for Becca's show."

"Oh... this is what you were talking to Mrs. Robinson about?"

"Yeah, we've been looking into expanding the chain to Seattle for a few months now. There's a gym there that is going bankrupt and we're going to check it out and see what condition it's in."

"If you buy it, would you guys be moving to Seattle?" Please God say no.

"No, we have enough resources now to just hire a few local managers to run the place for us, especially since this is already a gym and would not need a lot of renovations. We will need to go up there often at first, but we won't be moving. Plus we still need to open more here locally in California." *Thank you, Jesus!*

"Good!" I said a little too loudly, making Brandon raise an eyebrow at me. "What?" I smiled at him innocently.

"You don't want me to move, I take it?"

"Definitely not," I said, shaking my head with a smile. "Plus that would mean my weekly massages would end," I joked.

"Oh is that all you're using me for?" Brandon said, smiling.

"It is definitely one of the things."

"Oh really, Ms. Marshall? What other things are you using me for?"

"Well, I do need a good dancing partner occasionally." I smiled as I thought back to that unforgettable night in Vegas.

After dinner we went back to my place for the night. Even though I loved being at Brandon's, we discussed that we would switch off between homes. We'd have a little bit more privacy at his place and could keep Ryan company when we were at my place.

I think in the last week we both became accustomed to sleeping in the same bed with each other. I was already not looking forward to going to bed alone on Thursday night. How did I fall so hard and so fast?

It was now Wednesday and Brandon had his poker game tonight. After the gym he dropped me off at home so I could spend time with Ryan. After his game he was going to pick me up so we could have a night alone before he left Thursday morning.

Ryan and I ordered Chinese and watched TV for most of the night.

"Hey Ry, Brandon won't be in town tomorrow. You want to go to MoMo's for dinner and drinks after work?" I asked during one of the commercial breaks.

"I don't know. It's a weeknight." Whoa, when did that ever stop Ryan before? Okay, things were definitely worse than I thought.

"How are you ever going to meet someone new if you won't leave the house?" Operation "Get Max Back" had completely slipped my mind. I was kicking myself for not being a better best friend, but it had been a few weeks and I didn't think Ryan had heard from him. It was time to get her mind off of him.

"I don't know. I just really miss Max right now." I could see tears beginning to form in her eyes.

"Another reason we should go out and have drinks. We can have a good time and numb the pain."

"Fine, but if I don't want to stay out late, promise we can come home?"

"Promise."

〜

It was getting pretty late when Brandon finally arrived at my house to pick me up.

"Hey baby," I said while slipping into the car. Brandon leaned over to kiss me and I smiled. "Did you win tonight?"

He started to drive to his condo, "Kind of broke even. Did you have a nice time with Ryan?"

Throwing my head back against the seat I said, "Ah, her depression is killing me. She doesn't even want to leave the house anymore. I finally convinced her to go with me to MoMo's tomorrow after work. I plan on liquoring her up!"

"Oh, will I be getting drunk texts again?" he said with his famous smirk.

"Probably." This time if I said any of that stuff again, I wouldn't be embarrassed. Granted, I still don't think I could do the threesome thing. I wasn't sure I wanted to share him with anyone else.

When we arrived at his condo, Brandon led me inside and up the stairs to his bedroom. He immediately pulled me close to him and began taking off my shirt. "God, I am going to miss you," he said.

"You are only going to be gone a day, I'm sure it will be good for us." Good for my vagina anyway. It could use a little R&R. I mentally giggled as I gave him one of my own smirks.

"Tell that to my penis!" he laughed, making me giggle in return. Then he bent down, kissing me as his tongue brushed my lower lip and his right hand grabbed a small amount of my hair. Brandon easily lifted me off the ground and I wrapped my legs around his waist while our tongues danced together in passion.

Brandon sat on the bed with me in his arms. My legs were bent at my knees as I straddled his hips. I lifted his shirt over his head as he removed my bra. My panties were already dampening with my desire as I felt his cock swiftly harden in his jeans.

"Pants off now!" I said while I stood up to remove my own pants. Brandon removed his pants and boxers as I went over to his nightstand to grab a condom. "Lay down."

"So bossy, I like it!"

"Ha! I've never been like this before. Not sure what has gotten into me," I said, but actually I knew exactly what had gotten into me——this gorgeous man in front of me. I could spend twenty-four hours a day, seven days a week with him naked.

"I like it." And there was that slow, sexy smile again that melted my heart and made me want to do naughty things to him.

I crawled up his body and straddled him as I rolled the condom onto his already rock hard shaft. I returned my mouth to his and kissed him almost forcefully with need, making his cock twitch in response.

Breaking the kiss I turned around so my back was facing him. I held the base of his shaft as I slowly took him inside of me, inch by inch. My legs straddled him on each side, giving him only a view of my back. His hands grabbed my hips, guiding me.

My hands rested on his thighs and I started to move up and down. His hands reached up and caressed my breasts as my hips rocked hard against his cock. I swirled my hips as he met me thrust for thrust.

Our bodies rocked in sync as our hips moved with each other. I reached my hand down and rubbed my clit. Running my middle finger around and around until my pussy tightened and pulsed around his cock. Before my body was finished coming down from my orgasm, I felt Brandon's body go stiff as he thrust hard into me once more. "Fuck, baby," he said as he stilled.

The next morning was hard saying goodbye to Brandon. Even though he was only going to be gone for a little over a day, I was already missing him by the time I got home from work. I decided not to go the gym since I wouldn't have my workout partner with me.

While getting ready to go out to dinner with Ryan, I decided to text Brandon to see how his day went.

Me: *Hey Baby! How was your day?*

Brandon: *Hey Babe, it was alright. The owner was supposed to meet with us but he flaked. Pretty much a wasted trip, but we saw the place and the good news is that it isn't a dump! How was your day?*

Me: *It was okay. I think the article about your gym is almost ready to be put on the website! My boss thinks by our December newsletter that is emailed out. :)*

Brandon: *Awesome! Jason and I are about to head out for dinner. Are you still going out with Ryan?*

Me: *Yeah, I am getting ready now.*

Brandon: *Cool, call me tonight when you get home.*

Me: *Okay. It's going to be kind of weird falling asleep without you next to me tonight.*

Brandon: *I was thinking the same thing! I promise to make it up to you tomorrow night and this weekend since it is your birthday!*

Me: *Can't wait! I'll call you later.*

Brandon: *Oh Spence...*

Me: *Yeah?*

Brandon: *Last night was amazing!*

Me: *Just last night?*

Brandon: *You know what I mean! I might need to go out of town more often, if that is the sex I get the night before!*

Me: *Ha! Just didn't want you to forget me.*

Brandon: *You're not that easy to forget.*

Me: *Good! Have fun with Jason.*

Brandon: *Have fun with Ryan, and be safe, but I am looking forward to drunk texts! :)*

Me: *I'll see what I can do!*

I waited a few minutes until my face returned to its normal color.

"Hey Ry, you ready to go?" I said while walking out to the living room.

"Yep, let's do this shit!"

130

CHAPTER TEN

Ryan and I arrived at MoMo's and decided to sit at the bar again. The Giants had a day game and were not on TV, but it hadn't slowed down business one bit.

"What about that guy? He's cute," I said to Ryan while pointing at a guy at the bar.

"Eh, he's alright," she said disinterestedly.

Okay Ryan, you need to snap out of this shit! I rolled my eyes in frustration.

We were almost done with our second vodka cranberry and I was about to track down our waiter to order our third drink when I saw someone out the corner of my eye approach Ryan. Turning in her direction I saw that it was Max. *Fucking great, of all nights! Thanks, dude––I was trying to get her to forget your ass!*

"Max, what are you doing here?" Ryan asked, surprised.

"A few co-workers and I decided to come here for drinks after work." Max glanced over to me to give me a friendly hello smile. Fuck that shit! I shot him the look of death again and he had the grace to blush and awkwardly cleared his throat. "Can I talk to you...in private?" Max asked Ryan as he turned back to her.

"Um...." She licked her lips nervously and glanced from Max to me and back to Max again.

Don't do it Ryan, you haven't heard from him in weeks. Don't do it!

"Sure."

Damn it!

As Ryan started to get up from the table, I grabbed Max's wrist. My over protectiveness was in full force.

"Hurt her again, Max, and I swear to God, I will hunt you down, kick you in the nuts and make you sorry you ever met me."

"I understand, Spencer," he said gravely with a slight wince.

"We're good then." Smiling, I patted his hand and then let him go. I watched them walk out to the patio to talk and hoped again that they would be able to work things out. And I hoped Max wouldn't break her heart again. Because honestly, I had always really liked him and I'd hate to have to fuck his shit up.

~

They had been gone for about ten minutes and I was starting to get worried. As I was about to stand up, a guy approached my table. "Hey Courtney, how are you?"

Courtney? What the fuck? I looked up and my heart stopped when I realized it was Trevor from Vegas. *Shit!*

"Oh hi, Trevor, how are you?"

"I'm good, what brings you to San Francisco?"

"I'm in town on business, you?" *Oh shit, oh shit!*

"Yeah, same here. Where are you staying?"

Shit. What hotels are around here? Shit shit shit!

133

"Oh, I am actually staying with a friend. Killing two birds with one stone," I said with a nervous laugh. "Where are you staying?"

"The Wyndham at Union Square. But my co-worker and I went to the Giants game this afternoon and then we came here for drinks."

"Cool." We sat in a moment of awkward silence. "I..." just as I was going to excuse myself, Ryan and Max came back.

"Hey Spen..." My head quickly jerked in her direction, my eyes huge and probably bulging out of my head as I looked at her anxiously. Thankfully she noticed Trevor standing there before she finished saying my name. "Courtney... Phil is going to take us back..."

"Oh you guys are ready to go back to your place, Phil?" I asked. *Dear God, please let Max understand girl talk right now!*

"Hey Megan, it's nice to see you again," Trevor said.

"Oh you too, Trevor, how are you?"

"Great. I was just telling Courtney that we've been staying at the Wyndham while we're here on business. Is this trip business for you as well?"

I quickly answered for her. "Yeah, but we are staying with Megan's brother. This is Phil." Max's eyes widened and he mouthed "brother" as he looked at me questioningly. I just shook my head at him once and shot him a look that said, "Just play along!"

"Oh cool, nice to meet you, Phil," Trevor said and offered Max his hand.

Max hesitantly put his hand out to shake Trevor's hand.

"You, too. Trevor, was it? So um, yeah, are you girls ready?" Max asked, thankfully playing along. "I need to be at work early in the morning."

"Yeah, we are. It was nice seeing you again, Trevor," I said as I stuck out my hand to shake his.

"Likewise. Megan, should I tell Matt you say hi?" he grinned at her, innocent of his unknown faux pas.

Ryan looked like she wished the floor could have swallowed her whole as she said quickly, "Uh yeah sure, tell him I said hello. Hope you enjoy the rest of your trip. We've really got to get going though, so sorry!"

Oh dear God get me out of here. Never in a million years did I ever think I would see Trevor again and Ryan was a swiftly sinking ship. I guess that teaches us not to lie. Ha, who was I kidding? He still thinks my name is Courtney and that I live in Seattle.

As soon as we got in Max's car, Ryan and I said simultaneously, "Holy shit!" and sighed with relief.

"Max, even though I hate you right now, thank you so much for being here tonight!" I said as I buckled my seatbelt.

"About that, Spence. Max is going to drop you off and then we are going to go to his place and talk," Ryan said, turning around to face me in the backseat.

"Ok, no problem. I am just thankful to be out of that situation. That was so close!"

"You two want to tell me what that was all about?" Max asked.

~

When Ryan and Max dropped me off at home, I couldn't wait to call Brandon and hear his voice. It scared me how much I was already missing him. I settled into bed to call him and noticed I had a text message from a number I didn't recognize:

Unknown: *You should ask Brandon where he really is bitch!*

My heart sank. There were only five people that I knew of who knew I was dating Brandon besides Brandon and myself: Ryan, Jason, Becca and most recently, Travis and Misty. However, I am not sure if Travis and Misty even knew Brandon's name. Maybe Teresa from the gym, but that was highly unlikely.

I sat there staring at my phone, wondering what I should do. Should I respond? Should I call it and see who answers? Should I call Brandon and ask him whose number it was?

Brandon had never put any doubt in my mind that he wasn't telling me the truth of his whereabouts or even that he was seeing someone else. For the last week and a half, we had been together every night.

Since Brandon and I had started getting serious, I had told him everything about TravAss breaking my heart––no way could he be doing the same thing. Brandon even approached TravAss a few nights ago thanking him for being an idiot. There was no way...right? I took a few minutes to collect my thoughts. I couldn't be mad at him for something that wasn't true. I decided to call Brandon like we had planned. If he didn't answer, then maybe I had my answer?

My body relaxed when Brandon answered the phone on the second ring.

"Hey Baby." He had just referred to me as "Baby". No way could he be with another woman.

"Hi!"

"Did you and Ryan have fun tonight?"

"Yeah, but Max showed up and now they are at his place talking."

"Oh? That's good, right?"

"Ah, I guess. I really like Max but I hate what he did to Ryan. I threatened to make him sterile if he hurts her again!"

"You did what?" he asked while laughing.

"Yeah, I threatened to kick him in the nuts and make him sorry he ever met me." I was laughing, too.

"Aw Baby, you're such a good friend!" My heart skipped a beat when he said "Baby". There was absolutely no way he was out with another woman.

"I try. How is Seattle?"

"It's alright. I can't wait to be home and see you though."

"Me, too. What are you guys up to?" I have to admit that there was a hidden meaning to the question.

"We are just relaxing in the hotel room. Just got back from dinner."

"Tell Jason I said hello."

I heard Brandon say to Jason, "Hey, Spencer says hello."

All of a sudden, I heard a brief tussle and Brandon saying, "Dude, give me back my phone."

"Hello, Spencer!" Jason managed to say as I continued to hear commotion in the background. "Brandon is being a whiny little bitch right now because he can't wait to get back home." I laughed at Jason's antics and heard Brandon cursing and more tussle.

"Sorry about that. He's an imbecile." Brandon said after he managed to get his phone back.

"No worries. Well, I just wanted to say hi and let you know I'm home. I'm going to bed now."

"So no drunk texting?"

"No, not this time. We barely had two drinks before Max showed up."

"Damn," he said, sounding a little disappointed. "Okay then, I'll see you tomorrow."

"Night Babe, text me tomorrow?"

"I will. Oh, and I'll pick you up at six for Becca's show."

"Okay, sounds good. I'll see you then."

"Night Babe."

"Night."

CHAPTER ELEVEN

My Friday was a typical Friday. Brandon's flight got in at three o'clock and he sent me a text when he landed. I couldn't wait to see him. The rest of the afternoon crept along until it was finally quittin' time. When the bus finally dropped me off, I dashed into my house and quickly got ready for Brandon to pick me up. Becca's show wasn't starting until a little later, but Brandon and I were going out to dinner first. Ryan and Max had made up and were going to the show as well, but they were meeting us later at the gallery.

True to his word, Brandon picked me up right at six and took me to dinner at Jasper's Corner Tap & Kitchen. The mysterious, nasty text from the night before was weighing heavy on my mind. I knew Brandon wasn't lying to me, but I was also curious if he knew the number.

"So last night I got an interesting text from a number I didn't recognize." I didn't know how to bring it up casually, so I decided to just be blunt with him. No point in beating around the bush.

"Okay?" Brandon said while lifting an eyebrow.

I grabbed my phone and handed it to him. "I'll let you read it."

He glanced at the text and his eyes narrowed, his mouth tightening in a frown.

"You know who it is from?"

"Yeah, it's from my ex, Christy. Babe, I am so sorry about that. She has no right texting you."

"How did she get my number?"

"I have no idea... The only thing I can think of is when she came by a few weeks ago to pick up some things that she had left at my place before we broke up. I may have left my cell on the kitchen table and I left the room for a minute while I was getting her stuff. But Babe, you know I was really in Seattle, right?"

"Yes, of course! But I just don't understand why she would text me that."

"She's just trying to stir up trouble between you and me because she knows that she and I are over. I promise you that Jason and I were really in Seattle. I can even show you my boarding pass."

"Babe, I believe you. It's just odd that it came while you were out of town."

Sighing, he said, "I really didn't want to drag you into my drama. But since she's managed to involve you and now has your phone number, you deserve to know. Christy has been calling and harassing me every day since we broke up. Aside from the time when she came to pick up her things, I've pretty much been ignoring her calls. There have been a few times when I did answer because I was so angry with her. I have told her repeatedly to leave me alone and stop calling. I've tried being straight with her and telling her I've moved on and met someone else I am crazy about, but she just won't stop."

I nodded my head in understanding and grasped his hand in mine, squeezing gently. "I'm so sorry you've been going through such a rough time. I wish you had just told me to begin with."

"Like I said, I was trying not to drag you into my drama. I've been thinking about changing my number, but it is such a hassle and I really didn't want to burden you with all of this. I never thought she would go after you and try to break us up."

"I may have overheard you talking to her last Saturday morning."

"You did?"

"Yeah, but I didn't know she was harassing you. I still don't understand how she got my number though. Even if she got a hold of your phone, how does she even know about me?"

"All she had to do was read our texts and she could have figured that out. The only person I text more is probably Jason, but our texts are definitely of a different nature." He smiled at me, trying to put me at ease. I smiled back, but my stomach was still tied in knots.

Brandon and I finished eating and made our way to Becca's show. He was still noticeably upset. I had never seen him like that. Ryan and Max were waiting outside the gallery when we arrived.

Ryan was smiling like the old Ryan. She seemed happy now. And I was happy she and Max were working things out. I hadn't had a chance to speak with her about their talk but I guess it went well. I introduced Brandon to Max and they left to the bar to get us drinks.

As soon as they left, I turned to her to get the scoop. "So you and Max are back together?"

"Yeah. He said that these last few weeks have been killing him and he doesn't want to be apart from me."

"What about the whole kid situation?"

"He said he has changed his mind. Whatever I want, he wants. He wants a life with me." Ryan looked so happy that I hated to burst her bubble, but I wanted to make sure she was making the right decision.

"And you took him back just like that?"

"Spence, you know how much I love him."

"I know, I just hate how he broke your heart and now he can do it again. I only want the best for you, Ry."

"I know and I love you for that."

Ryan and I continued walking around the gallery. Becca's photos were gorgeous. She had photos that were taken in San Francisco and Austin. The photos she took in Austin had just been for fun but given her talent, she had to put them up. When they moved here to San Francisco, she took photography classes and decided to make it a career.

"So, Brandon's ex texted me last night."

"What? She did? What did she say?" Ryan asked as she turned toward me.

"She told me that I should ask Brandon where he really was last night."

"Oh my God, did you tell Brandon?"

"I did, that is how I know it was from his ex. He recognized her number." I shrugged.

"What did he say?" Ryan looked over my shoulder towards the bar behind me.

"He was worried that I didn't believe he was in Seattle and also told me that she calls him every day."

"Wow! What is he going to do?"

"I don't know. He said he would handle it."

Brandon and Max had returned with glasses of champagne. We continued to explore the gallery and I fell even more in love with Becca's photographs.

"I can't wait to get you home and out of that dress. I've been staring at your legs all night," Brandon said, whispering in my ear.

Blushing, I whispered back in his ear, "I can't imagine what would happen if you were gone for two nights, Mr. Montgomery."

"If that were to ever happen, we wouldn't be waiting until after whatever event we are at before I tear off your clothes. We would probably need to skip dinner," Brandon said, then kissed my cheek and pinched my butt.

148

We congratulated Becca and finally said hello to Jason who had been mingling with his wife before we arrived. Jason was beaming from ear to ear and I could tell he was very proud of his wife. Brandon was also proud of his friend.

We were one of the last ones to leave. Becca had a great turn out and most of her photos were sold. Ryan and Max were walking out with us and we were all going to head back to my place for the night.

We had all exited the gallery and were waiting for Becca to lock the doors when we were approached by a woman. She was taller than me, very skinny, with long straight blond hair, huge boobs, and a small mole on her right cheek that was barely visible; she looked like a model. *Great, another blonde.*

"What the hell, Christy?" Brandon snapped at her, clearly upset and agitated by her appearance. I froze dead in my tracks. Ex Christy?

"I need to talk to you," she said to him.

"Look, this is neither the time nor the place to have this conversation. I have told you hundreds of times that I don't want to speak with you. Leave me alone or I will file a restraining order...and stop harassing Spencer, too!" Brandon was angrier than he had been at dinner. He had let go of my hand and gotten up in her face, keeping himself planted firmly in between us.

Just as he started to turn away from her and reach for my hand again, she blurted out two words that made my heart drop to the pit of my stomach.

"I'm pregnant!"

"Pregnant? Did she just say pregnant?" I whispered to Ryan.

"Fuck!" was all Ryan could say.

I heard Becca gasp behind me. Yes, she said pregnant. I felt my legs giving out.

"And I care because?" Brandon said to Christy.

"Because it's your baby!" she snapped.

"Oh hell no!" I heard Jason say behind me, too.

"Ryan..." I said, still whispering to her.

"Yeah?" Ryan didn't even turn to look at me. Like me, our eyes were glued to the disaster in front of us.

"Pinch me."

"What?" she said as she finally looked over at me.

"Ryan, you need to pinch me. Like right now. Please wake me up! This can't be happening!" I was no longer whispering.

"What do you mean you're pregnant with my baby? We broke up weeks ago!" The volume of Brandon's voice was increasing in volume and was getting dangerously close to yelling.

"I'm six weeks pregnant."

"That's not possible."

Was this conversation really happening on the streets of San Francisco? I didn't know what to do. Ryan's arm was around my shoulders with her body pressed into my side holding me up. I felt like someone had punched me in the stomach; I couldn't breathe.

"I poked holes in all the condoms!"

"What the hell, Christy! Are you serious? That is some seriously messed up shit. Are you fucking crazy?" Brandon was pacing on the sidewalk, getting more and more upset. I could tell he was trying to keep his cool, but he was quickly losing that battle. I didn't blame him at all. If she wasn't pregnant, I think I would have punched her.

"I knew I didn't like you for a reason," Jason hissed.

"Christy, you are at my place of employment and before you cause a bigger scene, you need to leave. You and Brandon need to discuss this in private," Becca said as she stepped between Christy and Brandon.

"Babe..." Brandon said as he turned around to face me. "Ryan and Max are going to take you home. I will be there after I talk to Christy and straighten this shit out."

Brandon's knees were bent enough so that he was looking directly in my eyes as I felt them begin to sting with tears. Breaking away from my eyes, he looked at Max. Brandon kissed my lips and then Ryan tugged on my arm towards Max's car. My eyes blurred as they were still glued to the "movie" as I climbed in the backseat of the car.

～

When we got home, I collapsed on the couch. This was not happening. I didn't fault Brandon for this, especially if the bitch poked holes in the condoms. I was in love with him and I wanted to be with him. I just wasn't sure if I was ready to be a step-mother, especially since I wasn't a mother already.

"Spence, you want ice cream or vodka?" Ryan asked after settling in.

"Both! I want a double of each... together!" I said as my face was planted into the couch pillow.

"You want to talk about it?" she asked as she handed me my bowl of mint chocolate chip ice cream and a shot of vodka. She set the bottle of *Grey Goose* on the coffee table.

"Is this really happening?" I was struggling to hold back my tears as I tilted my head back while taking the shot of vodka that burned my throat a little.

"Yes, honey, it is," she said as she rubbed my back.

"But... how? After everything that Trav*Ass* put me through. I finally find someone who treats me good, who wants to spend twenty-four seven with me... who I am in love with!" I said with a big spoonful of ice cream in my mouth.

"You're in love with him?" By her question, you would think she would be shocked, but she wasn't.

"Yes, how could I not be?" I had just realized that Max was not in the room. I guess he wanted to give me space. He was slowly getting off my shit list.

"I know Brandon is a good guy, I can tell. This is just a very unfortunate situation." Ryan took the bowl of ice cream from my hands and set it on the table as she saw the tears rolling down my face.

"What do I do?" Heavy hot tears began to roll down my cheeks and soaked into the pillow I was now laying on.

"What do you want to do?"

"I don't know Ryan, this girl seems crazy. She fucking sent me that nasty text last night. She somehow got my number. How can I compete with crazy?"

"Honey, this is not a competition. I can tell and I know you can tell that Brandon doesn't want to be with that woman."

"I know but for the next eighteen years minimum he will have to deal with her. I know it is too soon to think this but... I will have to deal with her, too. Ahh, they don't have that saying 'baby momma drama' for nothing! This girl seems like a real nut job!"

"Do you want to be with him?"

"Yes, of course. This doesn't change how I feel about him."

"Then you have your answer."

"But..."

"No buts, Spencer. Just think, Brandon will be with you, not her. He will be holding your hand, cuddling with you and giving you amazing orgasms!"

"Ryan!"

"It's true! I have heard you," she said while winking at me.

"Oh great, this night just keeps getting better and better!" I said with a smile behind my tears.

"Spencer, I am your best friend, we are supposed to talk like this."

"I know, it's just embarrassing."

"Please, I know you have heard me and Max before!" *Ain't that the truth!*

"Yeah..." Before I could finish my thought, there was a knock at the door.

"Do you want me to get that for you?" Ryan asked.

"No, I'll get it."

I got up off the couch and had started to move towards the door.

"Okay, Max and I will be in my room, giving you time to talk. Let me know if you need me."

Ryan hugged me and then left. My heart was pounding. I had made up my mind that I wanted to be with Brandon, but what if he didn't want to be with me? I wiped my eyes and opened the door.

CHAPTER TWELVE

Before I could fully open the door, Brandon pushed it open himself. He pushed me against the wall, kissing me hard while his hands cupped my face. He picked me up and I wrapped my legs around his waist. Without breaking our kiss, he closed and locked the front door and walked to my room.

Entering my room, he closed the door behind him and slowly lowered me down so I was sitting on the edge of my bed. Brandon knelt down on his knees in front of me with his arms on each side of me.

"Spencer, I can explain everything. Please don't leave me."

"What? No..."

"Just let me tell you what I need to say." He looked directly in my eyes. I could tell he had been crying. "Nothing else matters except you, Spencer. Nothing. You're what I want, what I need. Where you are is *where I need to be*. I need you here in my life with me. Nothing Christy could ever tell me would be as important as you are to me. I'm going to love this baby and be the best father I can, but I want you there with me... I'm... I'm falling in love with you."

"You... you love me?"

"I do! I have never met anyone like you. I can't get you out of my head. You're all I think about every day. I hated being apart from you when I was in Seattle and that was only for one day. I can't imagine my life without you in it. Please don't break up with me."

"I love you, too," I whispered, still in shock. He told me he loved me. My head was spinning, but I felt the same way as he did. I had fallen in love with him, too.

"You do?" He actually sounded shocked.

"Of course I..." Brandon kissed me again.

Between kisses he started to talk again. "Spencer, after all the news... I have heard today... you just made me... so happy!"

Brandon unzipped my dress, letting it slip off my shoulders and down my body until it fell in a silky pool around my feet. He hooked his fingers in my panties as I laid down on the bed and lifted my hips. After stripping me of my panties, Brandon ran his fingers lightly through the hair of my pussy. I could feel the moisture building between my legs.

Leaning down over me, Brandon took my lips and his tongue started to make love to my mouth as if he couldn't get enough. I drank him in feeding my need, yet it did not remotely begin to quench my thirst for him. He gently sucked on my tongue as I moaned into his mouth.

Two fingers sank into me as his thumb created circles around my clit. I could feel them rubbing and stroking me, moving in and out. My core clenched as his fingers slid deep into my soaked pussy. As I was just on the brink of coming, Brandon stopped moving his fingers.

"Don't stop," I whispered.

"I know, Baby, but I need you to come around my tongue."

"Oh... oh!" Brandon's mouth was between my legs.

The heat from his mouth sent shivers up my body as his tongue dipped deep inside. I gripped the comforter as his tongue licked a path from the bottom of my pussy all the way back to my clit and then added pressure on my clit.

He increased his pace as his tongue dipped inside me again. My body clenched building up to an orgasm. His thumb circled my clit as his tongue deepened. I couldn't resist the pleasure anymore as my pussy clenched around his tongue as I screamed God and his name together. *Sorry, Ryan!*

I giggled as I realized that Ryan and Max had more than likely heard me.

"It's not really good for my ego if you laugh after I just went down on you, Babe."

I couldn't help laughing again at his slightly disgruntled expression. "Oh no, it was great. More than great actually. But just before you got here, Ryan told me that she has heard us before and then you made me just scream your name."

"Oh... I forgot they were here."

"It's okay, I have heard them plenty of times. We will probably hear them in a minute."

~

"Happy birthday, Baby!"

I looked at the clock and it was 12:01 a.m.

"Thank you!" I said as he leaned down and kissed me.

"I know we had planned to go to Santa Cruz today, but I was hoping that maybe we could just get away together——just you and me. After all of Christy's bullshit, I just want to be locked in a hotel room with you."

"Oh, I like the sound of that!"

"You think Ryan would mind?"

"I don't think so. I mean, she and Max are back together now so I'm sure they would enjoy some alone time. Plus I can do something Sunday night with her.... Where were you thinking?"

"I don't know... maybe.... Pebble Beach?"

"Oh, I have never been. That sounds perfect!"

⁓

We arrived in Pebble Beach around noon. Brandon had made reservations at The Inn at Spanish Bay.

"Checking in for Montgomery," Brandon said as we approached the Front Desk of the hotel.

"Yes, Mr. Montgomery, we have you checking in to an ocean view room for one evening."

"Yes, that is correct."

I glanced around the lobby as Brandon was checking in, taking in my surroundings. There were a few people relaxing on the gold colored couches that sat across from an unlit fireplace.

"Would you and Mrs. Montgomery like one or two keys?" *Mrs. Montgomery?* I stopped looking around and turned my attention to Brandon, curious how he would react to the clerk's assumption that I was his wife.

Brandon turned and looked at me while winking. "Two, please."

The clerk handed us our keys while Brandon grabbed my hand, tucking it around his arm. "Well come along, *Mrs. Montgomery.*" I blushed at his comment.

Our room had a spectacular view of the ocean. We had a balcony we could sit on which overlooked the golf course as it lined the coast. It was breathtaking. While looking out the sliding door to the balcony, Brandon came up and wrapped his arms behind me as he kissed my neck. "What do you want to do first, Birthday Girl?"

"I just want to relax and enjoy this view for a while."

"Okay, why don't we order room service for lunch and then tonight we can go to dinner for your birthday?"

"Sounds good to me."

I really didn't care. All I needed was here in this room. We ordered room service and opened a bottle of champagne that we picked up on the way to Pebble Beach. This was already turning out to be one of the best birthdays I have ever had. Despite recent events.

"Do you want to open your gifts now or later?"

"I have presents?" I was as giddy as a schoolgirl.

"Of course, it is your birthday...here, this is your small gift," he said as he pulled a long velvet box out of his duffel bag.

"Jewelry is a small gift?"

"Just open it, Spencer."

I slowly lifted the lid. Jewelry was a huge step. I knew we loved each other, but... "A key?" Okay, this was not what I was expecting.

"It's a key to my condo."

"Seriously?"

"Yep, I want you to come over whenever you want, even if I am not home... even when I am out of town."

"Wow, thank you!" I had never been given a key to a guy's place before. Trav*Ass* was my only serious boyfriend since college. He was apparently so wrapped up in himself and

Misty that he never wanted me to be unannounced. Come to think of it, I never really spent much time at his place.

"That's not all... here." Brandon pulled a big silver bag out of his bag that had white tissue paper stuffed in it to hide the present. "Sorry about the wrapping. I'm a guy."

"Aw, it's okay." I smiled at him.

While removing the tissue paper, I noticed a light brown, almost beige leather strap. Finally removing all of the tissue paper my breath caught when I noticed the famous monograms that lined the whole canvas material.

"Oh. My. God. You bought me a Louis? Oh my God––oh my God–– oh my God!" Now I really was giddy. I was jumping up and down, not hiding my enthusiasm.

"I did," he said with a wink.

"Oh my God, how did you know?" As soon as the words left my mouth I remembered...Vegas.

"Well, I felt bad when I won your money in Vegas so you couldn't buy your Louis."

"Ryan has a big mouth." We both laughed.

"Yes, but seeing how happy you are with your gift, I think I owe her." Grinning at me, he kissed my nose.

"I love it! Thank you so much. This is officially the best birthday ever."

"It's not over, yet, Spence." And there was the sexy smirk that always melted my heart and other things.

"Oh?" Brandon's mouth covered mine as his tongue slipped into my mouth. No matter how much we kissed, I could never get enough of his taste. His hand slipped under my shirt and cupped my right breast. I entwined my fingers in his hair and kissed him harder.

Before we could go any further, there was a knock at the door. It was room service. Brandon answered the door as I adjusted my shirt. While Brandon talked to the room service waiter, I slid open the balcony door and leaned on the railing, closing my eyes for a moment as I soaked in the beautiful sea weather. It was a warm day but not overly so. In a word, it was perfect.

"Your bacon cheeseburger and fries have arrived, my lady," Brandon said as he bowed.

"Why thank you, kind sir!" I said as I curtsied and giggled.

Brandon set our dome covered plates next to our glasses of champagne on the small table between the two chairs on the balcony. We sat there watching a few golfers play in front of us as we ate our burgers and fries.

I'm not sure how long we sat out on the balcony, but the sun started to set as Brandon cradled me in his lap with my head on his shoulder, my arms wrapped around his neck and my legs hung over the side of his knee. I didn't want to move, but I was sure Brandon was starting to get uncomfortable.

Just as I was about to get up and stretch my legs, Brandon asked, "You want to go have a drink by the fire pits?"

Out the back doors of the lobby, The Inn at Spanish Bay had fire pits that had a view of the ocean. There were five total with benches surrounding each one. The weather had turned cooler. It wasn't quite cold yet but I knew as the night went on it would get chilly.

Brandon and I were sitting on a bench that faced the ocean. His arm was around my shoulders as I snuggled into his side. I was drinking my go to drink, a vodka cranberry, while Brandon nursed a beer.

We talked to a young couple from Maine that was also there on vacation while we ordered another round of drinks. The lady was a nutritionist and I spoke with her about my company's website. Brandon and the man talked sports and at one point I heard them make a gentleman's bet about the Yankees and Giants playing against each other in the World Series.

After the sun had set, Brandon and I excused ourselves and went to dinner at Roy's, the hotel's restaurant. I ordered my favorite dessert, Crème Brulee, after we finished our entrees. Deciding to work dinner off, we took a walk along the path behind the hotel. My new Louis vibrated as we were heading back to the hotel. I grabbed my phone out of my purse to reply, assuming it was one of my friends wishing me a happy birthday. Only it wasn't.

Christy: *Don't think that just because he is with you now means he won't end up with me!*

This time I was able to recognize the number as Christy's. She was really starting to piss me off.

"Your baby momma is texting me again," I said, while handing Brandon my phone.

"God, when is she going to give it a rest?"

"Probably never." Honestly, women like that did not let shit rest until you were broken up. But there was no way that was happening. Brandon handed me back my phone. I started to put it back in my purse but realized he texted her back:

Me: *Christy, give it a rest. You're nothing to Brandon, he loves me and I love him. You're nothing but an incubator for his unborn child!*

"Oh my God you're bad!" I said while laughing and slapping Brandon on the arm.

"She is crazy. I still can't believe she poked holes in the condoms. Who does that?"

"Are you ready to talk about it?" The night air had turned chilly as a light breeze blew in my hair.

"I am ready whenever you want to talk about it, but it doesn't have to be now. I don't want to ruin your birthday." Brandon wrapped his right arm around my shoulder and rubbed my right arm when he noticed I shivered from the wind.

"Babe, it won't ruin my birthday. Everything that has happened today has been amazing! I love you so much and I want to talk about it. We *need* to talk about it."

"What do you mean *need* to talk about it?"

"I mean it's good if you talk about it. You can't keep it bottled up."

"I know. Fine, but we are taking a bath first. We'll talk later, I promise."

"A bath?"

"This room has a tub with jets, you're cold, I'm cold and I have been thinking about us taking a bath together, so that is exactly what we're going to do."

"Oh, I like the sound of that and I do need my butt warmed," I said with a wink.

The water was warm with bubbles overflowing the sides as Brandon and I stepped into the small oval tub. The tub was clearly made for one but we didn't care. Brandon's legs reached the top of the tub and my own legs rested on his ankles as I sat in front of him, my back reclining against his chest.

Brandon turned on the jets on the tub causing the water to ripple. I couldn't feel the jets as they were behind Brandon's back. Instead of enjoying the massage of the jets, he grabbed a bottle of my shower gel and squirted some into his hand. He returned the bottle to the left corner of the tub and began to rub the gel over my shoulders. The smell of French tulips, cherry blossoms and champagne filled my nostrils.

172

The gel began to foam as he continued rubbing the shower gel down my back. His right hand slipped to my front as he spread the foam around my right breast and nipple. I felt his cock starting to harden against my lower back.

His left hand glided across my left breast as he started kneading them both lightly in his hands. I bit my lower lip as I groaned. His hands glided down my belly as his erection grew even harder. His right hand continued down my body as his left returned to my breasts.

My legs spread a little wider as he parted his legs as far as they would go against the sides of the tub. His right hand started to massage my inner thigh as his left hand wrapped around my breast as he leaned me back against his chest.

The hand that was on my thigh began to rub my mound as his finger teased the lips of my pussy. Brandon kissed my neck as a finger slide into me. "Fuck!" I moaned as another finger entered. I closed my eyes as my hands gripped firmly on his thighs, the pressure slowly building. His thumb caressed my clit as his fingers slowly slid in and out of my center.

His cock throbbed against my back. I raised my ass a little off the bottom of the tub, my hands still gripping his thighs as I slowly moved up and down as his cock rubbed against my spine. Making waves, water splashed over the edge of the tub as I glided my back up and down over his length.

Brandon's fingers thrust harder into my pussy as his thumb rubbed my clit. "Don't stop," he whispered in my ear. Continuing to sway up and down our breaths became heavy with pants. I let out another groan as pleasure vibrated through me. Brandon kissed the top of my shoulder. "Let's move this to the bed."

We got out of the tub and before I could grab a towel, Brandon was tugging my hand and leading me to the bed. We were both dripping wet. I lay on the bed as he put on a condom. I wanted to tell him that he didn't need a condom because I was on the pill, but after Christy's news, I held my tongue.

Brandon approached the bed as I rose onto my hands and knees. He got on his knees behind me in the center of the bed and ran two fingers along the lips of my pussy. My body shuddered as my pussy was still sensitive from my orgasm.

174

I peeked over my left shoulder as his fingers gathered my juice and he ran his hand over his cock. He spit into his hand providing extra lubrication. The swollen head of his shaft inched closer to my pussy as it rubbed back and forth over the opening before he began to thrust inside me slowly. My head straightened towards the head of the bed as I arched my back in response to his cock filling me.

His hands gripped my hips as his cock slid farther into me. His hips thrust as his grip rocked my hips back, meeting him thrust for thrust. I reached between my legs as I steadied myself on one arm and began to massage my clit.

My fingertip circled my clit rapidly as Brandon's breath began to quicken. He pushed deeper into me again and again. I let out a moan as an orgasm washed over me. Brandon thrust a few more times and then groaned at his own release.

CHAPTER THIRTEEN

The comforter on the bed was still damp as Brandon and I crawled back into bed after a "real" shower. The night air had cooled tremendously and Brandon wrapped me in his arms to keep me warm while waiting for the heater to warm the room.

"Babe... I really wish I wasn't having a baby with someone else. I can't believe this is happening to me," Brandon said after a long sigh.

"I know. I can't believe it either. I know women are crazy, but tricking you into getting her pregnant is beyond crazy." I turned over so we were face to face, both lying on our pillows.

"I have waited my whole life to find 'the one', marry her and then start a family. I have always used protection, even when they told me they were on birth control. I just... I just can't believe this."

"I truly believe things happen for a reason. I'm not sure of the reason for this just yet, but I know you will get through this. Children bring joy into your life and I know you will be an amazing father."

"I just thought my life was starting to go the way I wanted it to go. Business is picking up, I don't need to worry about money and... I think... I have finally found 'the one'."

I literally thought my heart had stopped beating as my brain processed the words he had just spoken. "Me?"

Brandon rose and sat crossed legged in the bed. "I know we have only been dating a few weeks, but I have never felt this way about anyone. I'm not even sure how I made it through life before you."

I smiled as I sat up, wrapping my arms around his neck and kissing him on the lips. "Good."

"But really, Baby, I need you to help me with this whole pregnancy thing. I have no clue what to do."

"I don't either, but we will figure it out together. When is her next doctor's appointment?"

"She didn't say. I didn't ask. All she said was that she wanted me to pay for everything because she has no money to raise this baby since she quit her job."

"Doesn't she have medical insurance?"

"I don't know for sure, but probably not since she's still unemployed."

"Huh... well, find out when her next appointment is and we will both go."

"I love you, thank you."

I grabbed my phone to plug it in to charge and noticed that Christy had texted back. Sighing, I read the text:

Christy: *An incubator??? You fucking bitch! Brandon doesn't love you! You have only been dating him a few weeks cunt.*

Lovely. Ah, but she wasn't even worth my time anymore. Brandon sent the text, I knew how he really felt and she was just jealous that he was with me now. I didn't text back. Instead I crawled into bed and snuggled up to my man.

The next day we arrived back in San Francisco in the late afternoon. Brandon dropped me off at home and then went to his place to handle some business and get his things to stay over at my house again while Ryan and I went out to dinner for my birthday.

"Oh my God, Spencer, it's about time you got home!" Ryan said when I walked in the door.

"Um okay... I was only gone for the night, Ry."

"I know but I have something I have been dying to tell you... I mean, show you," Ryan said excitedly as she stood up from the couch and started walking towards me.

"Okay?"

"Look!" Ryan stuck out her left hand and a diamond ring shimmered in the sun light coming in from the window.

"*Holy shit*, Max proposed?"

"Yep." Ryan was smiling ear to ear. It seemed to be that breaking up with Max had turned out to be the best thing she could have done.

"I am so happy for you!" I gave Ryan a hug and then grasped her hand in mine, pulling it close to my face so I could check out the ring in more detail.

It appeared Max had spent a fortune on the ring. He, of course, had the money to do so since he was a Partner at a large firm that practiced all areas of law here in the city.

Ryan's ring was a single solitaire round shaped diamond that sat on a platinum band with five smaller round diamonds set along the center of the band on each side of the large diamond.

"Wow, how many carats is it?"

"Two."

"It's really beautiful, Ryan. Have you guys set a date yet?"

"Yep, May eleventh, our anniversary."

"Well, that seems fitting, but that is only eight months away. We better get planning!"

"And I want you to be my maid of honor, of course." I had assumed I would be, but it still made me feel good that she asked.

"I'd be honored," I said, squealing and giving her another hug. "I can't wait to throw you your bridal shower and bachelorette!"

I turned to go put my stuff in my bedroom when I heard Ryan ask me a question.

"Um wait a sec, Spence. Is that a Louis?"

"Oh yeah, it's my birthday present from Brandon."

"How did he kn... oh right, Vegas. Wow, he remembered."

"Yep, I'm lucky you have a big mouth," I said while winking at her and continuing to walk to my room. "Oh, and he also gave me a key to his condo."

"Oh my God. That's huge, Spence."

"I know," I said while smiling and continuing to my room.

∼〜

I decided that I wanted to go to MoMo's for dinner, which was quickly becoming one of our regular places. Since Brandon lived just down the street, he could give us a ride home.

We sat at the bar and we were enjoying our meal when I saw the devil herself walk in.

"Great, Christy is here," I said to Ryan.

"If she wasn't pregnant, I would kick her ass for you."

"If she wasn't pregnant, you'd have to wait your turn after me. Oh, let me show you the new text messages."

I showed Ryan the texts from Christy and Brandon's reply. We had a good laugh and when we were done, I glanced in Christy's direction and she was giving us the most evil look.

"You want to get out of here and head over to Brandon's?" Ryan asked.

"You know what? I want him to pick us up here."

"Oh, I love your thinking," she said as she clapped in agreement.

I grabbed my phone and texted Brandon:

Me: *Hey baby, mind picking me and Ryan up from MoMo's when you're ready?*

Brandon: *Of course, I'll be there soon.*

The next ten minutes were kind of painful. Christy and her friends eyed Ryan and me like we were the devil. However, she was the psycho bitch who poked holes in condoms. I wondered if her friends even knew the truth.

I saw Christy's eyes get big and I felt Brandon approach. He leaned down and whispered in my ear, "Trying to make someone jealous, I see." Before I could reply, Brandon leaned me back and kissed me hard with his left hand behind my head. My butt started to slip off the stool but he wrapped his right hand around my waist and supported me.

"Damn Brandon, knowing you get this worked up over making Christy jealous, I might just need to step up my game," Ryan said as we broke our kiss.

"You know, Ryan, a few weeks ago Spencer did mention a threesome."

"Ha! Not sure Max would agree to that you guys," I said.

After paying our tab, we were about to walk out of the restaurant when we were stopped by Christy.

"Hey Brandon, I need five hundred dollars for my first doctor's appointment."

"Christy, we already talked about this. You're supposed to send me an email listing your expenses and then I'll mail you a check."

Like hell you will. "Actually Christy, why don't you send him a copy of the doctor's bill and then he will send you half?" I knew it wasn't really my place to say anything, but I didn't like her just demanding things from Brandon.

"I've already paid for it, *Spencer*," she said with attitude, rolling her eyes at me.

"Trust me, the doctor's office can and will print you another copy. Have a nice night." I grabbed Brandon's hand and we left the restaurant with Christy staring at us.

We started walking towards Brandon's car that was parked on a side street. "Sorry if I overstepped, but I am not going to let her just come up to you and demand things anytime she sees you. She's obviously doing it to cause problems between you and me."

"No, of course. This whole pregnancy thing has fucked with my head. She knew I would just do whatever she wanted."

"Well, you asked for my help and I will not let her take advantage of you."

"And that's why I love you," Brandon said with another kiss.

"Get a room, you two!" Ryan called as she hurried to Brandon's car.

"We need to hurry. Spencer will be here soon," I thought I heard Brandon's voice say as I unlocked and entered his condo.

"Don't worry baby, I'll be fast. You know how you always make me come fast." *Was that Christy?*

I walked quickly down the hall and entered Brandon's living room. What I saw froze me in my tracks. Brandon's bare ass was in the air with Christy's legs wrapped around his waist. His hips rocked into her as her back squeaked against his leather couch and her finger nails dug into his shoulders.

"Oops, looks like we weren't fast enough," Christy said as she saw me over the back of the couch.

"Oh hey, Baby, come join us!" Brandon said. I just stood there, frozen in shock. I couldn't believe what I was seeing.

"Yeah Spencer, we can be one big happy family. Come here, sweetie. I've been dying to see what is so special about you," Christy said as she reached her arm out to me. Brandon continued to rock his hips into her as tears started to roll down my cheeks.

"Aw Baby, don't cry. This will be good for us. We can all live here and raise the baby together."

The room began to spin as I dropped to my knees. I started to hyperventilate as the tears continued down my cheeks and pooled on the floor.

"Aw, Baby, she is sad," Christy said. *No, you don't get to call him Baby!*

"What the fuck is going on?" I shouted. I couldn't see them as my eyes started to blur with tears.

Brandon pulled out of Christy and came over to kneel down beside me in all his glory. "Baby, Christy and I talked and I told her that I didn't want to leave you. So we came up with the plan for us all to be together. You will get me Mondays, Thursdays and Saturdays. Christy will have me Tuesdays, Fridays and Sundays. I will continue to have my poker nights on Wednesdays."

"What? You've got to be joking," I whispered raggedly, another sob catching in my throat.

"It's a win-win Spencer," Christy said. I looked up and wiped the tears from my eyes and I saw her huge grin.

"Like hell it is!" I said while shaking my head vigorously. "This is not what I want, not at all!"

"Baby, don't be like this," Brandon said as he brushed his fingers against my wet cheek. I cringed away, not even wanting him to touch me after his hands had just been all over her.

All I could say over and over again was no. This could not be happening. "Baby, why are you crying?" Brandon said as he continued to brush his fingers across my cheek.

"No, this isn't real, it's not. It can't be," I kept saying to myself.

"Shh Baby, don't cry, I'm here," Brandon said.

I shook my head, still crying, "No, no, no, no, no..."

"Spencer, wake up, you're having a bad dream."

"No, no, no, no, no..."

"Spencer, Baby, please wake up."

I gasped as I opened my eyes to see Brandon leaning over me.

"Shh, it's okay. You were having a bad dream, I'm here." I blinked at Brandon to try and focus on his face. I had been really crying as I slept through that awful dream and tears filled my eyes once more.

It was dark except for the light that was on my right side. I looked over and noticed it was from the lamp on my nightstand. "Baby, you're safe. I'm here." Brandon brushed his hand on my cheek.

"It... it was just a dream?"

"Yes, whatever it was, it was just a dream. You're safe."

I wrapped my arms around his neck and tugged him down to me. "It was just a dream" I repeated as realization started to become clear.

"Do you want to tell me about it?"

I told Brandon about my dream as he brushed his hand over my hair. "Baby, it was just a dream. I can guarantee you that will never happen. If I could, I would never see her again,

189

never talk to her again. I told you once before and I will tell you over and over. You are everything I could ever possibly want or need."

CHAPTER FOURTEEN

Over the next few weeks, I helped Ryan as she started to plan her wedding. Since she had been dreaming and fantasizing about her big day for most of her life, she had almost all of the details already planned out. We went dress and flower shopping, I helped send out save the date notices and we started planning her Bridal Shower and Bachelorette party.

Brandon and I continued our routine of working out four nights a week at his gym with one night always ending in the couple's massage room. My body loved the special treatment it was now getting once a week. Since Ryan and Max were back together and almost inseparable, we now spent most nights at Brandon's place. To my relief, I hadn't seen Christy again or received anymore texts from her. Maybe she was finally content enough to leave me alone now that she was getting Brandon's financial support.

Tonight was Ryan and Max's engagement party at her parent's house. Ryan's parent's lived in Atherton, which was about a forty minute drive from our house. Her parents had a six bedroom, five and a half bathroom mansion that sat on almost two acres of land. It was a New England style home with a gated entrance, three-car garage, tennis courts, a pool, and adjoining pool house.

When you entered the two-story home, you were greeted by a grand staircase that I always envisioned Ryan walking down in her prom dress to meet her date as a teenager. Their kitchen was similar to ours, except triple the size.

The kitchen led out to a tiled stucco patio that had a giant fountain in the center. Beyond the patio was a large pool that was surrounded by a large long yard that stretched the length of the house. Just beyond the pool was the pool house that also served as their workout room.

Ryan and Max invited only their closest friends and family to the party. However, there were still about one hundred people in attendance. Ryan also invited Jason and Becca and I was really looking forward to hanging out with them. I hadn't seen them since the night of Becca's show when Christy dropped the baby news bomb on us.

"You're not drinking tonight?" I asked Becca, who was out by the pool.

"No..."

"Oh, why not? The champagne is really good. Ryan's parents always get the good stuff."

"Jason and I are trying to have a baby."

"Oh my God, that is fantastic!"

"Sorry, I thought Brandon would tell you. Maybe Jason told him not to until we knew for sure."

"That's okay, I am so happy for you!" I said while I gave her a hug. "It's actually perfect because your and Brandon's kids can grow up together."

"I know, I am excited. I know Brandon isn't and I certainly can't blame you for not being, but I think you've been very supportive and he will be a good father."

"I think so, too. Just wish it wasn't Christy's baby. Has he told you about the texts?"

"Yeah, Jason told me. I would be livid if it were me," she said as she sipped her water.

"Well I'm not thrilled about them but I truly lov...like Brandon and want what's best for him and want him in my life."

"I know you love him. I can see it when you two are together. I have never seen him this happy in the...twelve years I have known him."

Brandon and Jason walked up as Becca and I were talking. I excused us so that I could introduce Brandon to Ryan and Max's parents and a few friends from college who I rarely saw nowadays. I showed Brandon around the house and Ryan's childhood room. There were posters of boy bands, famous actors and movie stars on her walls. Volleyball and tennis trophies rested on top of shelves that also held an array of books. Her parents kept her room exactly how she left it before college.

I turned to leave and reached out to grab Brandon's hand as he tugged me back. I stumbled into him, but he cushioned the embrace. I looked up into his eyes to question what he was doing when I saw the look in his eyes.

"Oh no, we are not doing it in here," I said as I tried to push him away. Not saying a word, he reached over and locked the door. "Babe, we *cannot* have sex in Ryan's childhood bedroom!"

"You're wearing the dress again," he said as his eyes lowered to my legs.

He looked around the room and then he took my hand and led me into the bathroom that was connected to Ryan's room. He flicked on the lights and locked the door. My heart began to race as I thought of Ryan trying to get into her room... or anyone else for that matter.

I lunged towards him and wrapped my arms around his neck as our lips met and our tongues swirled with passion. A fire always burned deep inside at just the thought of him touching me, kissing me, being inside of me. I broke our kiss as I ran my tongue along his throat and up the right side of his neck until I met the base of his ear. I sucked the end of his earlobe as he let out a groan.

His body pushed mine against the counter and he cupped my ass, pulling me tighter. His erection pressed into my mound as our mouths continued to devour each other. I reached down and grabbed a hold of the button of his jeans and slipped it through the slit. Slowly, I unzipped his jeans as his right hand cupped my breast through my dress, squeezing a little and sending need shooting down between my legs.

My breath and heart raced as I thought about how any second we could be discovered. I tugged on Brandon's pants when the zipper was fully down. He stopped my hands and yanked his pants down to his ankles. I slid my hand inside his boxers, grasping his thick cock, and began to lightly stroke it from the base to the tip and back down.

He slid me up on top of the counter and pushed my dress up to my hips. I spread my legs enough to allow him to step closer into me. Then Brandon stepped back out of my reach. He knelt down on his knees hooking a finger into the side of my panties and spread them to the side.

Closing my eyes, I leaned back against the mirror as he claimed me with his mouth, sucking, swirling and stroking the pink folds. My hands ran through his hair and I moaned shamelessly as his tongue darted in and out in an expert thrusting motion. Brandon continued to make love to me with his mouth until my pussy tightened convulsively. I moaned when a mind-numbing orgasm finally hit me, rocking my body with wave after wave of sensation. As he rose up and kissed me again, I could taste myself on him.

He grabbed my hips and lifted me off the counter, sliding me down until my feet touched the floor. Taking a condom from his pocket, he removed his jeans and boxers in one motion and tossed them on the floor. Then he sat on the closed toilet seat and pulled me over to him.

"Always prepared, I see," I said.

"Always, when I'm with you. I can't seem to get enough of you."

"Me either."

He motioned for me to come to him as I slipped my panties off and tossed them on the floor. I pushed my dress back up to my waist and straddled his hips, lowering myself onto him as he held his cock in his hand.

He closed his eyes as I used my legs to go up and down over his cock. "Fuck, Baby!" he said as he grabbed both of my ass cheeks. His hands glided up my back as I leaned into them causing my body to arch and his cock to hit the right spot.

My legs started to burn as I continued to ride his shaft over and over. I felt myself getting close to release. I looked at his face and knew he was close, too.

"I'm gonna come," I whispered.

"Me, too."

Brandon groaned as his body suddenly stilled, then he began to come. I slowly continued to ride him as my body tingled with pleasure. I sat completely up, with his cock still inside me, and rested my head on his shoulder. "I love you," I murmured.

"I love you, too," he said, and then kissed my left shoulder lightly.

We stayed like that for a few more minutes. I was sure I heard a knock as I lifted myself off of him. We quickly cleaned up and dressed. Exiting the bathroom, I heard another knock. I opened the door to find Ryan standing there.

"You *did not* just have sex in my old bed, did you?"

"Nope!" I said as we quickly exited her room towing Brandon by the hand.

"Good, because I might have to kill you if you had."

We all started laughing as we walked down the stairs into the foyer.

～

Two days later, I woke with a sinking feeling in my stomach. On my lunch break Brandon and I were going with Christy to her doctor's appointment. I, of course, was going to support Brandon. I had no intention of speaking with Christy—— I didn't even want to look in her direction.

My plan was to remain in the waiting room while Brandon and Christy went in to meet with the doctor. To our surprise, Christy wouldn't let Brandon in the room. She told him and the doctor's assistant that she was not comfortable with him in the room. This might work out better since I would probably have a million things running through my head with them in the exam room and me waiting.

Brandon and I sat quietly in the waiting room while Christy was being examined. I looked around the room that was filled with children's books, pregnancy magazines and toys. I never imagined myself sitting in a room like this and not being pregnant.

Brandon's hand clenched mine as his right leg bounced up and down. I could tell he was nervous and anxious. I was trying not to show how nervous I was. The receptionist and other assistants whispered behind the front desk, giving us furtive glances. I figured it wasn't every day that the girlfriend of the baby's father went to the appointments. It wasn't like I had demanded to be in the exam room or anything.

Christy finally exited into the waiting room and she and Brandon settled the appointment fee. When we stepped out into the hall she shoved the ultrasound into Brandon's chest. "Here!" she said and continued to walk down the hall. Brandon and I stopped and looked at the black and white ultrasound.

We stared at the picture for a few minutes not saying anything. A little oblong object was surrounded by a dark circle; the dark circle was surrounded by lighter shading. Baby Montgomery with the date and time was on top of the picture.

Looking at the tiny person stilled my heart. It was a piece of someone who I loved, but not a piece of us. I wanted to cry as the realization began to sink in. Was I really ready to help raise someone else's child? Someone who wished I didn't exist?

I looked up at Brandon, his eyes were glossed over. "You made that," I whispered. He looked up from the picture into my eyes. I could tell his heart was breaking––this was not what he wanted. I wrapped my arms around his neck as we both cried into each other's shoulders.

Brandon dropped me off at work. I wanted to spend the rest of the afternoon consoling him, but my boss would only allow me to take a long lunch. She was working on a deadline and needed my help.

I kissed Brandon lightly as I exited his car. We were both quiet on the drive over and didn't say anything as I got out of the car. There were no words. We both knew we didn't want this. There was nothing he could do about it and I wasn't ready to leave him over it.

I stepped into the bathroom before heading to my desk to freshen up my make-up. I didn't want all my co-workers asking me what was wrong. They didn't know my situation, only that I was happy and dating someone new. When I finally made it to my desk, I placed my cell phone down on my desk just as Brandon texted me:

Brandon: *I love you!*

Fighting back tears again, I texted back:

Me: *I love you too!*

CHAPTER FIFTEEN

The next couple of nights, Brandon and I stayed at his place. On Wednesday he went to poker night but didn't stay long. He was still shaken up by the ultrasound. I knew once he held the baby in his arms, he would fall in love. I bought a picture frame for the ultrasound and placed it on the desk in his home office. I also put a framed picture of myself on his desk so he would remember I was always here for him.

I was cooking dinner when Brandon's phone rang. His face lit up, something I hadn't seen since Saturday night at Ryan's engagement party. "Hi Mom," he said as he answered his phone.

"I'm doing good, how are you and Dad?... You are?... When?...This Sunday?... Yes, of course, I can't wait to see you... I have someone I want you to meet... Yeah, it is really serious... Her name is Spencer... Yes, she is a girl... Mom, I will tell you all about her when I pick you and Dad up from the airport... Okay, I love you too, tell Dad hello... Okay, bye."

When Brandon was talking to his mom about me, he would look over in my direction and smile. I missed that smile. "So my parents are coming this Sunday and staying the night. They are flying to Hawaii on Monday morning," he said from the couch in the living room.

"That's awesome! When was the last time you saw them?"

"Christmas."

"Wow, it has been a long time."

"Yeah, they are really busy. My dad is trying to retire though."

Brandon's dad was in real estate. He was very successful in the Houston area, but the last few years had been tough with the economy. Though from what Brandon had mentioned before, they were still well off financially like he was.

"I can't wait to meet them," I said.

Meeting the parents was a huge step. I started to get nervous. What was I going to wear? What if they didn't like me? Great, now I was nervous and stressing myself out.

"Spence... they... they don't know about the baby." Sorrow returned to his face.

I turned off the burner on the stove and walked over to where Brandon was sitting on the couch. I knelt down in front of him, grabbing his hands in mine and looked up into his eyes. "They will love this baby just like I will because it is a part of you. They are going to be so happy to be grandparents and like all grandparents, they will spoil your baby."

Brandon had mentioned to me before that he had a younger brother who didn't have kids either, nor was he married. Since Brandon was thirty, I figured his parents would be happy to finally be grandparents.

"I hope so. They raised me to get married first and then have kids."

"Babe... this is not your fault. You didn't do anything wrong. Once they know what Christy did, they won't be upset. I don't know them but I believe they will accept this baby because it is your baby."

"I hope so."

"I know so."

~

When Brandon's mom called him, I realized I hadn't spoken to my own parents since my birthday and then only briefly. The last call prior to my birthday had been when I told them that Trav*Ass* and I had broken up. I usually talked to my mom at least once a week, so I wondered why she hadn't called me.

I called my mom and everything was fine. She said that she was just giving me time to mend my broken heart. I told her all about Brandon and that my heart was completely mended. I didn't mention the baby. I wanted them to meet Brandon and fall in love with him first before I mentioned the kicker about our relationship.

My mom was happy for me although a little worried that I was moving too quickly into a new relationship. But she said she couldn't wait to meet Brandon. She and my dad were not able to come to Ryan's engagement party because of financial reasons, so they decided they would just come to the wedding in May. I told them I would be flying down for Thanksgiving and might bring Brandon. I didn't know if he was going to Texas for the holidays or not, but I needed to see my family.

⁓

On Sunday Brandon went to the airport to pick up his parents. Brandon asked me to wait for them at his place so they could catch up a little. I dressed in jeans with a light grey sleeveless blouse that had ruffles down the front, a turquoise cardigan and light grey calf high boots. Brandon assured me I looked adorable and his parents would love me before he left.

When Brandon left he was all smiles -- finally. I nervously walked around the condo, tidying things that really didn't need tidying. I heard Brandon and his parents walk in as I was in the kitchen getting a glass of water. I turned around from the fridge when they walked into the living space.

"Mom, Dad, this is Spencer," Brandon said as I walked over to them, meeting them half way. Brandon wrapped his arm around my shoulders.

"Spencer, these are my parents, Robert and Aimee."

"It is so lovely to meet you!" his mom said. I went to shake her hand but she pulled me in for a hug.

Brandon's mom was my height, curly light brown hair with bangs, a few freckles kissed her cheeks and she looked really young for her age.

"You too," I said, then turned to Brandon's dad to shake his hand.

He shook mine in return and gave me a smile. I knew now where Brandon got his smile from. "Yes, it is so good to meet you," he said.

Brandon looked almost like his dad. They had the same smile, same eyes and similar builds. His dad was a little shorter than he was, but you could tell they were father and son.

After our meet and greet, Brandon took their bags up to the second bedroom. I spoke with his parents about how

Brandon and I met... leaving the dancing part out. His dad was impressed that I knew how to play poker.

When Brandon returned from putting their bags in the room, his dad mentioned to him that we should have a poker game tonight. Brandon was excited with the idea. His face lit up and he texted Jason and a few other friends I hadn't met yet who he played with on Wednesdays.

After dinner, we were all going to play at Brandon's condo. He was beaming from ear to ear; this was exactly what he needed.

After a glass of wine and getting to know each other, his parents excused themselves and went to lie down for a few hours before dinner. With the time difference, they said they needed a nap before they would be ready to stay up all night playing poker.

Brandon and I rested as well. The last few days had been emotionally draining and we were both exhausted. I fell asleep with Brandon rubbing my back. When I woke, he was wrapped tightly around me. I didn't want to be anywhere else but in his arms.

〜

We took Brandon's parents to The Waterfront Restaurant for dinner. After his parents finished their first glass of wine and were starting their second, he told them about the baby. At first they both sat there staring at Brandon. Finally his mom spoke.

"I'm... I'm finally going to be a Grandma?" she asked. I could tell she was happy. I felt my whole body relax and Brandon loosened his grip on my hand as he relaxed.

"Yes," Brandon answered.

His mom stood up and rushed around the table and hugged Brandon. My heart melted. I knew they couldn't be mad at him. His dad hugged Brandon as well. They were excited. I think finally Brandon was excited as well. When they all returned to their seats, his mom asked the million dollar question.

"When is she due?"

Brandon and I looked at each other, our eyes wide and eyebrows arched. We had no idea; Christy never told us. I tried to quickly calculate the timeline in my head.

"Well, I think she is almost ten weeks now. So... I think the second week of June."

Brandon's face returned to panic. I think his mom realized and she quickly expressed how delighted she was and couldn't wait to be a grandma.

The rest of dinner went well. We talked about the baby, my work and Brandon and Jason buying the new gym in Seattle. His parents wanted to meet Christy but knew it wouldn't be on this trip. I was happy. The less I saw of her the better.

After dinner we went back to Brandon's condo and not long after we arrived, Jason and Becca showed up. We were setting up the poker table when three of their other friends arrived. Brandon introduced me to Ben, his contractor who remodeled Club 24; Jay, a personal trainer at Club 24 and Vince whom he and Jason met through Ben.

We decided to play tournament style Texas Hold'em and all throw in twenty dollars. Whoever was the last one standing would take it all: one-hundred and eighty dollars. Brandon's mom was out first, followed by Becca and then myself. Like in Vegas, Brandon took me out. I made a plan that I was going to practice and next time take him down... hard and maybe with better winnings, like a full body massage.

While the guys played, we girls chatted and became cocktail waitresses. I was getting along really well with his parents. I could tell that they were good people. Vince was out next and became the permanent dealer. Not long after that Jason was out.

The rest of the guys decided to take a ten minute break. Brandon came over to me where I was sitting on a stool and wrapped his arms around me from behind and kissed me on the cheek.

"Are you having a good time?" he asked.

"Well, I would be having a better time if you hadn't taken all my money again!" I said, laughing.

"I know of ways you can earn it back." The smile that melted my heart and did other wonderful things to me finally reappeared.

"Oh? I like the sound of that!"

After the break the guys returned to playing. Not long after, Ben and Jay were out, leaving Brandon and his dad. Ben, Jay and Vince all stayed and drank beers with the guys as we ladies continued talking and serving drinks. I felt like I should have started demanding tips after a while.

After what seemed like another hour, Brandon finally lost. His dad took him down with pocket Queens. I had a sneaky suspicion Brandon let him win. Brandon had only a pair of eights and they weren't even pocket eights.

Everyone hung out and helped clean up, and then we all said our goodbyes. Brandon's parents retired to their room and Brandon and I went to his room.

I started to undress in the bathroom and was about to jump in the shower when Brandon came in to do the same.

"Babe, your parents are here!"

"So? They are down the hall and we are adults, not teenagers sneaking around, Spence."

"I know. It's... it's just weird."

"It will only be weird if you aren't quiet." Ah and there was that smile again. I thanked my lucky stars for it being back. "Plus we took power naps earlier; you can't be tired, Baby."

I was tired, but with him being in such a good mood, he could make me do anything just with that smile.

We undressed and stepped into the latte colored tiled shower that was big enough for two. There was a seat on the right end when you stepped in. Brandon sat down there.

"What are you doing?" I asked.

"I just want to watch you for a little bit."

"Um... okay."

The warm water ran down my hair and back as I leaned my head back wetting my hair with my body facing Brandon. Once it was completely damp, I began to massage some shampoo into my hair. I looked over at Brandon, his eyes were dark with desire, his cock long and hard making my belly clench.

I bit my lower lip as I rinsed the shampoo from my hair. Next came the conditioning step, followed by another rinse. I closed my eyes as I tilted my head back under the water, letting the warmth stream down my face. I had to shave my legs, but I'd never done it in front of anyone before. First time for everything, I supposed. Moving closer to where Brandon was sitting, I placed my right leg up between his thighs, resting my foot on the built-in bench.

I shaved my right leg as he peeked several times between my legs. When I was done with my right leg, I did the same to my left. Brandon reached out to touch me between my folds. "No touching," I said while giggling and slapping his hand.

"You're killing me, Spence."

"Hey, you're the one who wanted to watch," I said with a wink.

After I was done shaving my left leg, I squirted some shower gel in my hands and started to soap myself, my hands sliding over my breasts until it began to lather. Brandon and I stared at each other. He grabbed his cock in his right hand and began to stroke himself. I spread the lathered suds down my belly inching my way down to my pussy.

Before I could get any further, Brandon stood. "That's enough of that," he said with clenched teeth.

We both stood in the streaming warm water and I rinsed my body free of the soap. Brandon spun me around so I was facing the side wall and ran his hands down my shoulders, to my breast, down my belly and then my pussy. He stroked my clit as I bit my lower lip trying not to moan.

I pressed my left forearm against the shower wall to support myself as I leaned over and spread my legs wider. Brandon ran his hands down my smooth legs as he kneeled down on the floor behind me. I raised my right leg and placed it on the built-in seat.

Brandon was the perfect height for running his tongue between my folds. Two fingers filled me as he pushed them up and down inside my pussy and flicked my clit with his tongue over and over until my body found its sweet release.

We each stepped out of the shower and grabbed a towel, wrapping them around us. Brandon led me to the bed and threw both of our towels on the floor. I scooted back in the bed as he retrieved a condom from the nightstand and slipped it on.

He crawled into the bed and hovered over me as he kissed me on the lips and traveled his mouth down to my breasts, sucking on them. My back arched in response as I bit my lower lip against another moan. Brandon rose up a little and then filled me with one swift move, impaling me with his hard, throbbing member.

My arms circled his neck and my legs locked together behind him as he thrust again, deep inside me. He returned his mouth to mine as his tongue and cock worked together, bringing my body to shatter again as I climaxed. He thrust hard into me a few more times until he found his own sweet release, clenching his ass under my ankles as he came.

217

We both returned to the bathroom, Brandon to shower, and me to blow-dry my hair. Then we crawled tiredly into bed, wrapped up closely in each other's arms and drifted off to sleep.

CHAPTER SIXTEEN

The next morning when Brandon and I woke, we made his parents breakfast before they had to leave for the airport. Brandon dropped me off at my house first and then took his parents to catch their flight. Having them here for just one night was the best thing that could have happened. *My* Brandon was back.

Ryan and I had our usual plans to go shopping for Halloween costumes and then carve pumpkins like we did every year. This year we decided we wanted to be sexy civil servants. She was going to be a fireman and I was going to be a police officer. Every year since living in this house, we would always pass out candy and then afterwards go to a party. This year would be no different. One of Ryan's co-workers always threw a huge Halloween party no matter what day of the week it fell on.

After our torturous afternoon at the Halloween store, we went to a local pumpkin patch and each picked out two pumpkins. We were not the only ones who waited until the last minute to get costumes or pumpkins. Both places were packed with customers. Luckily we were both able to find what we wanted.

"Max is coming over to watch the game, right?" I said to Ryan as we set the pumpkins on our dining room table.

Tonight was game four of the World Series. Our *San Francisco Giants* were up three games to none and had a chance of sweeping the *Detroit Tigers*. Unfortunately, the game was being held in Detroit so we had to watch them on the TV while we carved pumpkins.

"Yep, Brandon too, right?"

"Yeah, I just need to text him to let him know we are home. What time is Max coming over?"

"He should be here soon. I already texted him we were home."

I texted Brandon to let him know I was home. Not long after, Max showed up with a twenty-four case of *Blue Moon* beer.

"Let's get this party started!" he said when he walked in the door.

Ryan slapped him on the arm and told him he was silly. Finally everyone in my life seemed to be back to their normal selves.

"I'm going to put on some sweats so my nice clothes don't get all messy from the pumpkins," Ryan said as she started to walk to her room.

Finally, this gave me an opportunity to ask Max about the girl I saw him with at Fog City Diner a little over a month ago. I never told Ryan that I saw him. I wasn't sure if it was breaking the friendship code, but I didn't want anything to cause her anymore heartache. Also she was finally happy again and that was all that mattered... right?

"Hey, Max, can I ask you a question?" I asked, whispering so Ryan couldn't hear.

"You just did," he said with a laugh.

"You know what I mean." I couldn't stop my eyes from rolling at him.

"Yeah, sure, what's up?"

"Who was that girl I saw you with at Fog City Diner?"

Max came closer to me so he could whisper, "I know what you're thinking, Spence, but that was my sister, Melissa. You know I love Ryan. After she left me, I was torn up. I really didn't know how badly she wanted kids."

"Oh..." I forgot his family lived in San Francisco, too.

"Look, it took a couple weeks for me to realize what I had, I admit it. Those weeks were the hardest weeks of my life. Every day I thought about Ryan, every day I tried to forget about her, too, but you know how hard she is to forget. Finally, I was tired of going to bed every night thinking of her only to wake up the next morning still thinking about her. I knew what I had to do. I talked to my family, I hung out with my nieces and nephews and I realized I wanted that, too... with Ryan."

He seemed sincere and I really wanted to believe him.

"She didn't look happy at MoMo's that night you saw me, and I knew it was my fault. I didn't know how I was going to get her back and when I saw you two there, I just went for it."

"Went for what?" Ryan said as she entered the kitchen.

"Oh... um..." Max couldn't say anything.

"Your ring, Ry. He was telling me how he picked it out," I said, covering our asses.

"Oh. Don't you just love it?" she said as she showed me again for the hundredth time.

"Yes, I do, you lucky bitch!"

A few minutes later Brandon came over with steaks and then he and Max headed out to the backyard to grill them for dinner. Meanwhile, Ryan and I worked together in the kitchen, making a salad, baked potatoes and garlic bread to go with the steaks.

"So you liked Brandon's parents?"

"Yeah, I liked them a lot. They were really sweet."

"Did you guys tell them about the baby?" Ryan always got to the point quickly and never shied from asking the hard questions.

"Yeah, Brandon did."

223

"And?"

"And, they took it really well. His mom is really excited about becoming a grandma." I chopped more greens for the salad and then tossed it with a light vinaigrette.

"Is Brandon doing better now?" she asked, turning to the oven with a fork to check on the baked potatoes.

"Yeah, I think so. Seeing his parents really helped. He was so devastated after seeing the ultrasound. I guess he just hoped it wasn't true."

"I think we were all hoping it wasn't true."

"I know," I said, sighing.

The game started shortly before dinner was ready. We all sat in the living room crowding around our coffee table while we watched the game and ate dinner. The game was so good that after we cleaned up from dinner, we moved one of our couches and coffee table and set newspapers down so we could carve our pumpkins and watch the game at the same time.

Since Ryan and I carved them every year, we had a book that contained patterns with funny faces, scary faces, witches, cats, etc. and all the carving tools. Ryan chose to do a pumpkin with a witch that was flying on a broom in front of a moon. I chose to do a crescent moon with a face with a bat flying in the center of it like it was flying over it. Brandon chose to do the Grim Reaper's face and Max picked a haunted house on a hill with bats flying around it.

I went to change into sweats while they continued to set-up the living room. When I got to my room I realized I had a missed text message. I opened it and saw that it was from Christy. When was she going to leave me alone?

The text message read:

Christy: *You actually think I am going to let you help raise my baby bitch?*

I didn't respond. I just tossed my phone on my bed and changed my clothes. She really wasn't worth my time; however, I just wanted to put her in her place. How was I the bitch? Why was I the "bad guy"? I knew I would love this baby like it was my own. And maybe that's what she feared.

After a couple of hours of drinking beer and carving our pumpkins, we munched on freshly roasted pumpkin seeds as the Giants won the World Series four to three. Our pumpkins were complete. I was feeling really good after my fourth beer and I could tell Ryan was, too. We had each only had four beers whereas Brandon and Max each had six. This was the first time that Brandon was buzzed around me. I had never seen him drink so much.

Buzzed Brandon was very talkative and not really about anything in particular. It was sort of cute. He also couldn't keep his hands off of me and Ryan had to tell us a few times to go to my room. I just slapped his hands off of me and we continued carving our pumpkins.

Our pumpkins didn't turn out perfect like we had hoped. Alcohol, sharp tools and straight lines didn't mix well. Halfway through, Brandon had to help me finish my pumpkin and Max had to help Ryan. We weren't very good at the details.

Ryan's witch was flying on a crooked broom and her moon was not a perfect circle. My crescent moon was wavy and the bat was flying kind of sideways and almost into the moon's eye. Brandon did better on his pumpkin; however, his Grim Reaper's eyes were lopsided. Max did better too, only his bats were flying crookedly; his house was kind of perfect though.

It was getting late and after we calmed down from the Giants winning, we decided to call it a night as we all had to work the next morning. When I came out of the shower, Brandon was passed out naked in my bed. I guess he was tired of waiting for me. I crawled in bed with him and stared at him for a few minutes.

I loved everything about this man. He was perfect for me. How was I going to help raise a baby? Brandon didn't even know what to do and looked to me for guidance. Did Christy even know how to raise a baby? She quit her job out of laziness and boredom, so she was not exactly role model material.

That night I had another nightmare. It wasn't like my previous one. I didn't cry in my sleep and Brandon didn't wake up. I dreamed that we were all accused of being bad parents and the baby was taken away by Child Protective Services. I guess that is what happens when you fall asleep thinking about being a bad parent.

～

Today was finally Halloween, which fell on a Wednesday this year. Normally I would dress up for work but this year was a little different. Because the Giants won the World Series on Sunday, most of San Francisco took the day off and enjoyed the celebration parade. The news channels estimated that Market Street would be packed with over a million people to watch the parade.

Max's law firm was located on Market Street so we watched the parade from his office. It was an awesome day and the only thing that could have ruined it was if we had bumped into TravAss in the office. Thankfully that did not happen.

After the parade, Brandon dropped me and Ryan off at home. Then he left to check on the gym and head home to get ready for his poker night while Ryan and I headed to her co-worker's Halloween party.

I told Brandon that I would meet him at his condo after the party. I had something special planned for later when I arrived at his condo.

Ryan and I started to get ready for the party around five o'clock. My cop costume was a button down blue fake cop shirt and elastic blue shorts that matched. It came with a fake badge and a plastic holster that held handcuffs, a water gun and another pouch for my keys, I.D., money and cell phone.

Usually around 6:30 p.m. the little kids from the neighborhood would come by trick or treating, and Ryan and I loved to see their cute costumes as we handed out candy.

When trick-or-treaters started to come around, we took turns opening the door. I opened the door several times to find the most precious children standing in front of me. I started to think that this time next year I might be Trick-or-Treating with Brandon and his baby or we could at least dress him or her up as a pumpkin and take a picture that would last a lifetime.

KIMBERLY KNIGHT

Ryan noticed that I was starting to get emotional. "What's wrong, Spence?"

"Just thinking about next year at this time."

"What do you mean?"

"You know, Brandon and his baby––where we might be. What if I am no longer in the picture?"

"Just like you have told me before numerous times, all you can do is take one day at a time."

"I know. I just kind of wish it was my baby."

"You do? You barely know him."

"No, I know. It's more the fact that it isn't my baby. I just wish it was a piece of us, *not* just a piece of him."

"Just like you tell me all the time, everything happens for a reason."

"Thanks, but that is not helping!"

"Look Spence, it's only October. Christy isn't due for eight more months. You have eight months to decide if this is

230

what you want. You don't need to make the decision tonight. Let's just finish giving out our candy and go get *drunk.*"

And that is exactly what Ryan and I did. We finished handing out all our candy by nine o'clock and "sexified" our costumes by adding heels, more make-up and hoop earrings.

We took a cab to Ryan's co-worker's house and drank multiple glasses of the adult punch with gummy eyeballs floating in it. We ate hot dogs wrapped in a crispy Phyllo that looked like mummies, bread crostinis in the shape of ghosts with a jalapeno artichoke dip, mini slices of pizza with mozzarella on the end and cheddar around the crust that made it look like candy corn and a few cupcakes that had different Halloween decorations on top.

We weren't sure if it was because Halloween was on a Wednesday or if people were still out celebrating the Giants, but there were not that many people at the party this year. Ryan and I only lasted an hour and a half before we were bored. We took a taxi to Brandon's condo and she continued on to Max's house.

I said goodnight to Ryan and headed up the elevator to Brandon's condo. I stepped out onto his floor and took my fake handcuffs out of the leather pouch on the holster.

I knocked on the door instead of using my key. While I waited for Brandon to come to the door, I leaned my right hand on the doorframe and twirled my handcuffs around my left pointer finger.

Brandon opened the door and before he could say anything I said, "I've heard you've been a naughty boy, Mr. Montgomery!"

CHAPTER SEVENTEEN

"Yes, Officer, I have been naughty but I heard that you've been even naughtier."

"Oh? How is that?" I asked as I stumbled a little into the condo and shut the door behind me.

"I believe you were drunk in public outside and there is a fine for that in California."

"Well, Mr. Montgomery, you are correct. So what is my punishment?" I asked as I bit my bottom lip and batted my eyelashes playfully.

"First you need to hand over those handcuffs and sit in a chair in the dining room so I can interrogate you."

"Don't you need to arrest me and read me my rights first?"

"I'm not a police officer so this will be a citizen's arrest. Now sit down, Officer Marshall."

"So bossy," I said as I walked into what was considered the open lay-out dining room, pulled the chair out at the head of the table and sat down. I gave Brandon the handcuffs as he held his hand out to me.

"Now, Officer Marshall, put your hands behind the back of the chair."

As I sat in the chair, I reached my arms around the back. Brandon walked behind me and cuffed my wrists together. He bent down and whispered in my ear, "I'll be right back."

"What? You're just going to leave me like this?" *This was not part of the plan.*

"I'll be right back, Officer Marshall."

He ran up the stairs taking them two at a time. A few minutes later he returned in only his boxers. In his hands were the ties from my robe and his robe, a towel and a condom.

"What are you going to do with the ties?"

"You'll see," he said with that smile. *Fuck.*

My panties were instantly damp and I could smell my arousal. I could see his erection trying to escape from his boxers causing me to bite my lip as I thought of all the pleasure that was in store for me.

"Lift your butt," he said as he stood in front of me.

I obliged and he put the towel on the seat and I lowered my butt back down when he had finished.

"I think this interrogation will be conducted better if you didn't have those shorts on, Officer Marshall," he said as he slid the elastic band of the shorts down my hips and hooked his fingers in my panties, taking them down together and then tossed them on the floor.

He took one of the robe ties and tied my left ankle to the left front leg of the chair. He did the same to my right leg causing my legs to spread, exposing me to him. He cupped my mound with his right hand as he bent down and kissed me. I could taste beer on his breath as our tongues swirled around each other.

235

He rubbed my mound and brushed one of his fingers over the lips of my pussy. "God, you're already so wet, Baby."

"Uh huh," was all I could say as we continued to kiss.

"Scoot your hips down to the edge of the chair, Baby," he commanded and I eagerly complied.

Brandon knelt down on his knees as he leaned down and ran his tongue up my pussy, licking all of my juices that had begun dripping out of me. I threw my head back as the sensations rippled through me. He continued using his tongue skillfully until my body convulsed. I let out a frustrated moan as I tried to close my legs to ride out my orgasm.

He continued using his tongue and started using his fingers until I climaxed again... and again... and again.

With my eyes closed, I felt Brandon release my hands from the fake handcuffs. I opened my eyes as he came back around and untied the ties that bound my legs to the chair. He gestured for me to stand as he held out his hand. I took his hand and stood. Then he unbuttoned my shirt, threw it on the floor, unclipped my bra and tossed it onto the pile as well, leaving me completely naked.

He removed his boxers and sat in the chair I was sitting in. I continued to watch as he rolled the condom onto his cock. "Come here, Baby," he said.

I walked the few steps to the chair, lifted my right leg up and over his left thigh and did the same with my left leg as I hovered over him continuing to stand. He held the base of his cock as I inched down and he filled me slowly.

My pussy was raw and sensitive from the multiple orgasms, but I didn't care. I took all of his length until it filled me completely. I hooked my left arm around his neck and placed my head on his left shoulder and rocked my hips as I slid up and down.

Brandon lightly stroked my back as I moved up and down. I could tell that he was already close to coming because after only a few more strokes, I heard him hold his breath and felt his body clench as he exploded into the condom. I wrapped my arms around his neck and kissed him until I could no longer breathe.

~

As it got closer to Thanksgiving, we made plans to fly down to Encino and spend Thanksgiving with my parents. The Wednesday before Thanksgiving I worked a half a day at work and then Brandon and I headed to the airport. Brandon didn't seem nervous about meeting my parents. I, on the other hand, was freaking out inside. I had never brought a guy home before. Trav*Ass* always made an excuse when it involved meeting my parents. Looking back on our relationship, I couldn't believe I never saw the signs.

My mom and dad picked us up from the Burbank airport when we arrived. My parents pulled up to the curb and Brandon put our luggage in the trunk as my mom got out of the passenger side and hugged me for dear life. It had been almost a year since I had seen them. When we got into the car, I introduced Brandon to my mom, Julie, and then to my dad, Kevin, who was driving.

During the hour-long car ride in Los Angeles traffic, we caught my parents up on the last few months since Brandon and I had been together. We didn't tell them about the baby. I didn't want to give them a reason to not like him and this was not Brandon's fault. I would tell my parents when the time was right, but the first meeting was not it.

We finally arrived, parking on the street in front of my childhood home. I had always loved the one story house which was currently painted a light blue with white trim. Brandon and I put our luggage in my room where we would both sleep in the same bed. My parents were not naïve. They knew I wasn't a virgin and had to assume Brandon and I were sleeping together, even though they would never discuss it with me. My room was still decorated pretty much as I had left it when I went to college, just like Ryan's parents left hers.

The summer after college when I came home, I took down all my teen heartthrob posters and put up a few framed black and white photographs of Europe that I had bought at

Target. There was one of the Eiffel Tower in Paris, one of Big Ben in London, and one of a vineyard in Tuscany.

That night I helped my mom brine the turkey and make pumpkin and pecan pies while Brandon and my dad got to know each other. I had no doubt they would get along. In a lot of ways, they were alike. My dad was always our protector and I knew deep down that Brandon would not let anything hurt me.

"So, Brandon seems really nice," my mom said as she rolled out the pie dough.

"You have no idea."

"He is the first guy you've brought home you know."

"I know and it was his idea, too."

"Really? Sounds like the opposite of Travis."

"What do you mean?"

"Come on, Spencer. You were with him for a long time. What was it... two years? I know you didn't come alone all those times because you didn't want us to meet him."

"You did?"

"Well, look at your sister. She's only been with Chris for a year, but we've already seen him a few times."

"They live in Thousand Oaks, which is much closer than San Francisco," I laughed.

"I know, but still, I was just hoping I would meet him prior to your wedding and not at the wedding," she said sarcastically.

"Ha! Wedding. I don't think Trav*Ass* will ever marry anyone but himself."

"Trav*Ass*?"

"Oh," I giggled. "Ryan came up with that nickname and I kind of adopted it."

"I like it," my mom said as she winked at me.

⁓⁓

My sister and her boyfriend, Chris, came over for Thanksgiving dinner around noon. At one o'clock Brandon, my dad and Chris were getting ready to watch the *Dallas*

Cowboys game while we girls remained in the kitchen getting all of the food ready. Well this was another cliché.

"Brandon is *hot*, sis!" my older sister, Stephanie, said.

"I know and he is all mine, so back off," I said as I pretended to threaten her with the knife I was holding.

Stephanie and I were really close growing up. Since we were only two years apart, we tended to crush on the same boys and fought like crazy. Since she had gone to UCLA after high school and I had moved to Santa Cruz two years later, we had drifted apart. Of course, we kept in touch, but thankfully we had each found our own guys.

Chris came into the kitchen looking for snacks and beer while we continued to prepare our feast. I walked towards the living room and overheard my dad and Brandon talking.

"Yes, sir, I do love your daughter."

"I worry about her being up there in San Francisco."

"Sir, you don't need to worry. I won't let anything happen to her."

"Please, call me Kevin, and I think I trust you. I never met that Travis guy, but from what I heard, he could give two shits about Spencer."

"I have met him and I will never treat Spencer the way he treated her. You have my word."

"You seem like a really nice guy, but if something happens to my baby girl...let's just say I have friends."

I heard them both laugh.

"Kevin, I love your daughter very much and hopefully one day we will all be family."

"You want to marry my daughter? It's my understanding you have only been dating a few months."

"I do want to marry her, but I know it is too soon. But I don't see my future without her in it. She is like my rock. She is smart, funny, the most beautiful woman I have ever seen, a good dancer..."

"Brandon, you don't need to get all girly on me. I get it. But you have been warned. Now let's go see why it's taking Chris so long with those beers."

I hurried down the hall I was standing near and into the bathroom so they wouldn't see me. I was fighting back tears after hearing what Brandon told my dad. I couldn't believe it. After all these years a guy... a great guy wanted a future with me.

The rest of the evening went well. Everyone was in a food coma after all the food we ate. Brandon's Cowboys ended up losing by seven points and he was crushed. We played poker and just like all the other times, Brandon won my money. He also won everyone else's money and I made a mental note to practice on my lunch breaks or something.

We stayed until Sunday afternoon. My parents really seemed to like Brandon. I think at one point I overheard my dad calling him "son", which made me feel all warm and fuzzy inside.

The next few days flew by. On Tuesday, Brandon mentioned that he and Jason had to fly to Seattle again on

Thursday and wouldn't be back until the evening on Friday. They were going to sign all the papers to buy the new gym, so we made plans with Jason and Becca to go out Friday night for a celebratory dinner.

Wednesday after Brandon's poker night, he came over and we stayed at my place so I could do laundry. I had a ton of it. Brandon had cleared a space in his closet for me, but he didn't understand that I had a hard enough time deciding what to wear with all my clothes being in the same place.

We actually had our first fight because of it. It wasn't a heated fight, just a disagreement. We ended up compromising with me going shopping this coming weekend for more clothes since apparently I needed to fill two closets now. I stopped arguing. I was a girl after all and loved shopping. Now my boyfriend was demanding I have more clothes. I didn't even know that scenario existed.

Brandon had already moved some of his clothes into my closet and a drawer in my dresser. He was lucky as he had a much simpler wardrobe. For work he just dressed in jeans and his Club 24 polo shirts, and on the weekends he would wear jeans and a t-shirt. He only really dressed up if we were going out somewhere that required it.

Thursday morning Brandon drove me to work and then headed off to meet up with Jason before they left for Seattle. It wasn't even lunch time and I was already missing him. Just knowing that I would not see him was killing me. I couldn't even imagine if it was for more than one night. I started to scare myself at how attached I had become to him in such a short amount of time.

Thursdays were usually our days to get massages at the gym. Brandon made me keep my appointment, and after work I headed to the gym to get my massage. Everyone at the gym greeted me by name and was very genuine. I hoped it wasn't only because I was the boss' girlfriend.

After my massage I changed in the locker room and headed out the front doors to catch the bus home. Without looking I ran right into someone. As I stepped back to apologize, I realized it was Trevor from Vegas again.

"Oh, excuse me," I said as I looked up to his face.

"It's always a pleasure running into you, Courtney."

"Oh, um... hi Trevor." *Fuck.*

"Back in San Francisco?"

There are only a certain amount of times that you can lie before it catches up to you. And I was just about done with this particular game. I wasn't going to tell him my real name or that I had lived in San Francisco the whole time, but I figured I should at least confirm that I did live here now.

"Actually, I just moved to San Francisco," I replied, answering his question.

"Did you get transferred for your job or something?"

"Yep, sure did."

"That's ironic. I just moved to San Francisco." *Shit.*

"Oh really? Why?"

"Let's just say there is nothing left for me in Washington."

"Oh okay, well, it was nice seeing you again but I really need to catch the bus."

247

"Why don't I give you a ride home? Maybe we can grab dinner and a drink first?"

Now what was I going to do? My luck he would follow the bus until he saw me get off just so he knew where I lived.

"You know, actually tonight is not a good night. I really need to head home; I have a lot of unpacking to do still from my move."

"I can still give you a ride home."

"You know, Trevor, I need to be honest with you. I have a boyfriend, so I don't think that will be a good idea. I really need to go. Take care," I said while I ran off to catch the bus that was pulling up to the corner.

I sat in the back of the bus and watched out the right side window as Trevor got into his car. He didn't go into the gym, which made me wonder why he was even there. The bus started down the street and I looked out the back window and noticed Trevor didn't follow. Relief washed over me.

I finally made it home and told Ryan what had happened. She called Max and repeated everything to him and he came over to stay the night with us instead of Ryan going over to Max's. I didn't mean for Ryan to change her plans, but I didn't want to take the chance if Trevor had indeed followed me home.

I decided to call Brandon to tell him the whole story. I told him about how Ryan and I met Trevor in Vegas, how he had bumped into me at MoMo's once and then how I ran into him at our gym today. Brandon was concerned and told me that if anything like that ever happened again, to turn back around and go into the gym and talk to whomever is at the front desk or go up to his office and call him.

We talked a bit more and he told me how his day went in Seattle -- how he and Jason met with the bank and started the procedure to buy the gym. Ben, Brandon's contractor, had met up with them in Seattle to discuss the remodel that was going to take place and how soon the gym could open. They were shooting for the first day of the New Year. It should be a huge success with everyone and their New Year's Resolutions.

Friday morning Brandon and Jason were going to finalize everything and then head home. I couldn't wait to see him. Brandon made me feel safe and all I wanted was to be in his arms.

After we hung up, Ryan, Max and I watched TV and planned more of their wedding. Ryan *told* Max which tuxedos he and his groomsmen needed to rent and we talked about having the bachelor and bachelorette parties in Vegas in April.

That night I tossed and turned in bed. I was definitely not used to sleeping alone anymore. I woke Friday morning exhausted. I grabbed my cell phone as I was heading out the door to catch the bus for work. I noticed that Christy had sent me a text during the middle of the night. *Of course she did.*

Christy: *Are you ready?*

What the fuck did that mean? I stuck to my guns and I didn't reply to her messages. I didn't want to stoop to her level and be petty. Honestly, if she kept this up, I was just going to change my number.

At lunch, my boss took me out for a special treat to celebrate our December newsletter which featured her article about Brandon's gym:

December 1, 2012

By Skye McAdams

Club 24 is an up and coming chain of gyms that recently opened their latest location in the San Francisco area on September 1st of this year. It is owned and operated by Mr. Brandon Montgomery and Mr. Jason Taylor; both native Texans. Mr. Montgomery and Mr. Taylor opened their first location in Austin in 2005. After the success of their Austin location, these savvy businessmen opened a Houston location in 2007.

Mr. Montgomery and Mr. Taylor continued their success by making their way to the West Coast, first opening another branch in Denver in 2009 and then more recently in San Francisco a year ago. It is my understanding that on January 1, 2013, they will open their newest branch in Seattle.

What makes Club 24 unique is the atmosphere. Not only do they have state of the art exercise equipment, but each treadmill, elliptical, stair climber and exercise bike provides its own 12" personal TV for your viewing pleasure.

Club 24 offers several free classes: Kickboxing, Yoga, Kenpo, Zumba, Cycling and Aerobics. You can also find weekly beach volleyball games being played in the custom outdoor beach volleyball court.

If you are looking to learn new moves or find out how to get beach body ready, you can hire one of their accomplished personal trainers for as many sessions as you need at a reasonable price.

After you work up a good sweat you can cool down by jumping in the lavish indoor lap pool or soak your achy muscles in one of the three hot tubs near the pool. If you're looking to sweat out more toxins in your body, you can relax in one of the two saunas.

Club 24 also offers a full service spa, complete with a barber shop for the gentlemen and a salon for the ladies. You can also tan for free in one of the UV free custom airbrush booths or in one of the "instant" tanning beds. It is called the "instant" bed because it has been known to instantly get heads turning after use. The tan will show up hours faster and last days longer than other tanning beds. With this complete 360 *degree tan you will not only look sexy but feel sexy too.* **WARNING: May cause lots of compliments and flirtatious looks after use!**

After spending most of your day working on your fitness and relaxing those muscles, check out the cafe complete with a juice bar and coffee shop.

Make Club 24 your second home. I know I am!

~

Shortly after I returned from lunch I remembered that I left my only nice dress at Brandon's condo. It was the same dress that I wore to Becca's show and Ryan's engagement party. I giggled to myself thinking this was exactly why I needed to go clothes shopping this weekend. I wasn't going to tell Brandon he was right and I did need enough clothes to fill two closets.

After work I took the bus to Brandon's and texted him that he should pick me up there instead of at my house:

Me: *Hey Baby, I'm almost to your place. I left my dress there so you need to pick me up at your condo. Miss you.*

253

Brandon: *I miss you too. Just landed, we should be there in about 45 minutes and then we will go to pick up Becca. Be safe and lock the door!*

Trevor slipped from my mind the whole day. I didn't think to look around and see if he was following me. I locked the door once I was in Brandon's condo and ran up the stairs to take a quick shower. Forty-five minutes wasn't very long so I needed to hurry.

When I got out of the shower, I heard the front door close. That was fast. I quickly put on my jeans and t-shirt so I could peek out and tell Brandon I wasn't ready yet. I knew Jason was with him and I didn't want him to see me in my robe.

Just as I came out of the bedroom to run down the stairs, I saw the person walking up them. It wasn't Brandon.

CHAPTER EIGHTEEN

"What the hell are you doing here?" I hissed at Christy when I saw that it was her and not Brandon walking up the stairs.

"I came to *talk* to you."

"How did you even get in here?" My hair was dripping down the back of my black t-shirt and onto the floor.

"I have a key," she said with a smirk.

Christy was standing at the top of the staircase only a few feet from me as I stood in the doorframe of Brandon's bedroom.

"Why do you have a key?"

"I had one made while I was with Brandon."

"Oh... so he doesn't know?" I asked with attitude in my voice and crossed my arms over my chest.

"No, and you know what, Spencer, I am not here to make small talk with you," she snapped.

"Well, why the *fuck* are you here then?" I could feel my blood start to boil.

"I'm done with you standing in the way of Brandon and I being together..."

"Me standing in the way? He doesn't want to be with you, Christy!" I shouted as I cut her off and dropped my arms to my sides in protest.

"Before you came into the picture we were happy. We were going to get married!" she yelled back.

"Oh really? Did he propose to you?" I asked as I crossed my arms over my chest again.

"Well... no."

Christy was standing there like we were friends having a normal conversation and not moving any further than the top of the stairs. This bitch was batshit crazy and really starting to piss me off.

"Then how are you so sure you were going to get married?"

"I just had a gut feeling that he would have proposed soon if you hadn't entered the picture and spoiled everything!"

"That was your gut telling you that you were going to get dumped," I said as I giggled a little.

"Fuck you, bitch! This ends now. It's time to get you out of the picture." Her face had turned bright red as she yelled at me.

"And how are you planning on doing that?" My blood was on fire and my hands were shaking with anger as I dropped them to my sides again.

"I'm going to kill you!"

"You're wha.." Christy started to reach behind her back and I saw the light from the window above the stairs reflecting on something shiny. Before I could fully catch a glimpse of what she was pulling out from behind her back, she lunged towards me with her right hand out. The shiny object was a knife.

I jerked my right shoulder back and barely avoided the knife that was headed straight for my chest. Christy almost fell when her knife missed me. I quickly backed up towards the stairs and Christy lunged at me again. I continued to rotate in a circle as she almost fell again.

"Christy, calm the fuck down – you're acting like a crazy person! You didn't think this through!"

"The hell I didn't! I have been planning this for weeks," she said with an evil laugh.

Christy and I were rotating in a circle like a school yard fight. My fight or flight instinct had kicked in and I chose fight. I watched the knife in her hand, waiting for her next lunge.

"So your plan is to kill me and you think that Brandon won't hate you for the rest of his life?"

"Brandon won't find out."

"How is that? We are in his fucking condo!"

"I brought *help* and items to dispose of your body."

It took me a few seconds to process what she had said. We continued to spin slowly. Was this going to be it? Was I going to die? Would I never see Brandon again?

"What about all the blood? How are you going to clean it up before he gets here?" I asked, trying to buy some more time while I tried to think my way out of this crazy situation.

"Like I said, I have help." She lunged at me again. My back was at the top of the stairs. I bent my legs as I twisted again to the right. Christy missed me again, but this time she fell down the stairs.

I stood at the top of the stairs watching as she slid facedown with her arms reached out in front of her, clenching the knife in her right hand. Before she met the bottom of the stairs, her body curled up into a ball and continued to tumble down the stairs with her head facing the handrails.

When she finally met the bottom level, I saw the knife sticking out of her stomach. Blood began to seep through her blouse and onto the floor. Her eyes were closed and she wasn't moving.

I stood there for a minute or so just staring at her in shock, waiting for her to make the slightest movement. She didn't move. I ran into Brandon's bedroom and grabbed the cordless phone on the nightstand and dialed 911.

"911, what is your emergency?" the dispatcher asked.

"Someone broke into my boyfriend's condo and we fought... and there is blood everywhere!" I shouted into the receiver.

"Ma'am, calm down. Is anyone hurt?"

"Yes."

"Are you or your boyfriend hurt?"

"No...I am here alone with her." Tears started pooling in my eyes as I began to cry.

"Is the intruder hurt?"

"Yes, yes she is. There is blood everywhere and she isn't moving." Tears were rolling down my cheeks. I wiped them but the tears continued to roll down my cheeks.

"Okay, Ma'am. Help is on their way. Are you safe at this moment?"

"I... I don't know. She isn't moving."

"Okay, I am going to stay on the phone with you until help arrives. If you don't feel safe, please lock yourself in a room. Help will be there any minute."

"Okay... thank you," I sniffled.

I watched Christy as she just laid there with her eyes closed. Her blood had started to pool around her body. A few seconds later I heard the faint sound of the sirens in the distance.

"I hear the sirens," I told the dispatcher.

"Yes, Ma'am, they should be arriving in less than a minute."

"Okay, thank you. I need to call my boyfriend."

I hung up before the dispatcher could respond. I needed to call Brandon. I didn't know how long Christy and I fought but I was expecting him at any minute. I sat on the first step at the top of the stairs looking down at Christy's body.

"Hey Baby, Jason and I are just down the street. There is some commotion with cops and fire trucks so we are stopped in traffic to let them pass."

"Bra...andon..." my voice cracked.

"Spencer, what's wrong? You never use my name."

"I... I think... I think I killed your baby." I started to cry again as the words left my mouth.

"What do you mean?"

"Christy broke in..."

"She what? Stay there, I am almost there." I heard Brandon tell Jason that Christy had broken in and then I heard the car door open and a lot of white noise, like he was running.

"Baby, I am literally like a block away. Are you hurt?"

"No." I sniffed again.

"Where is Christy?"

"She is lying on the floor not moving, there is blood everywhere."

"Stay with me on the phone, Baby. Just keep talking to me until I get there." I could tell Brandon was running. He wasn't out of breath but he sounded a bit winded.

I started to tell him how Christy used a key that she made and entered the condo when I was getting out of the shower. Before I could go any further, firemen and paramedics were entering the apartment. I looked down at them where they were standing by Christy's body. Stunned, I stared at them for a moment, unsure how they had gotten in. Then I realized that Christy had probably left the front door open.

I hung up with Brandon. He said that he was getting in the elevator and a paramedic was walking up the stairs towards me.

"Ma'am, are you hurt?"

"No," I answered as I looked up at him.

I clenched the phone in my hand as the paramedic turned around and walked down to Christy's body. I sat there staring as the paramedics tended to her.

Brandon ran into the condo a few seconds later. He paused for a brief moment looking at the bloody scene. He looked up at me, our eyes met and he was instantly bounding up the stairs to wrap his arms around me, hugging me tight.

263

"Thank God you're okay. Tell me what happened," he said as he continued to hug me, holding the back of my head firmly with his right hand and with his left arm wrapped around my back.

I pulled my head back glancing at Christy and back at Brandon as I started to retell him what had happened. Before I could finish again a police officer and Jason walked up the stairs.

Brandon and I continued to sit on the top step of the stair case as I told the police officer what had happened. Jason leaned on the railing a little behind the police officer and listened to my story while Brandon rested his arm around my shoulders to comfort me.

While I was relaying everything to the police officer, the paramedics put Christy on a gurney and took her to the hospital. She was alive. We told the officer that she was pregnant with Brandon's baby and he said it was up to me if I wanted to go to the hospital to see how she was doing.

I could tell Brandon was torn. I made the decision easy for him. I didn't want to stay alone and I knew he needed to check on his baby. I left Brandon and Jason as I went to Brandon's room to finish changing so we could go to the hospital.

I put my bra on and put back on my black t-shirt that I wore that day for casual Friday at work; the back of the t-shirt was still damp from my hair. I put on my San Francisco Giants pull-over sweatshirt that I had hanging in Brandon's closet and slipped on my dark grey *UGGS*.

Pulling my hair back, I wound it into a loose knot on the crown of my head, but I didn't have the energy or willpower to put on any make-up. I didn't want to go out in public looking like a mess even though inside I was trembling.

Jason left to pick up Becca when Brandon and I left for the hospital. He said they would meet us there. I asked Jason to call Ryan for me and he said he would as he gave me a hug.

When Brandon and I arrived at the hospital, we checked in with the Emergency Room and were told to wait until a doctor could give us an update on how Christy and the baby were doing.

We waited and waited. Jason and Becca arrived followed by Ryan and Max. I recounted the horrific event as Becca and Ryan gasped several times. Everyone hugged me numerous times as they were thankful I wasn't hurt. Brandon never let go of my hand.

Finally, after waiting several hours, a doctor came out to talk to us. She was reluctant to talk to us because we weren't family but we only had one question for her.

"How is the baby, doctor?" Brandon asked.

"Baby?" The doctor paused and checked his chart. "I'm sorry - I can't give you any information. You will need to speak with Ms. Adams regarding that."

CHAPTER NINETEEN

Brandon and I turned to each other searching for answers. Why was there a question after the word "baby" when the doctor answered Brandon? I heard our friends gasp and start whispering to each other.

"Please Dr. Ames, just tell me if my baby is okay," Brandon pleaded.

"Sir, I wish I could tell you more; however, due to patient-doctor confidentiality, I am not able to give you any information. You'll need to speak with Ms. Adams."

"Well, when can we see her?" Brandon asked.

"Visiting hours are almost over for the night and Ms. Adams is in the Post Anesthesia Care Unit. She will not be able to have visitors until tomorrow at eight a.m."

We thanked the doctor and turned to our friends who were sitting behind us.

"How much you want to bet that she's been faking the pregnancy all along?" Jason said.

Ryan, Becca and Max agreed with him. Brandon and I didn't say anything and then I remembered about the ultrasound.

"But... she gave us the ultrasound..."

"Yeah, we went to a doctor appointment with her and saw the ultrasound," Brandon said, agreeing with me.

"Is it possible she faked that, too?" Becca questioned.

"How can you fake an ultrasound?" Ryan asked.

"You would be surprised at what people are capable of. I have seen some crazy shit at my law firm," Max said.

"But we were there at the doctor's office," Brandon said.

I just stood there listening to everyone. I didn't have the energy. Not only had Christy tried to kill me tonight, but now she may or may not have been pregnant this whole time.

"Guys, can you take us home? I can tell Spence is tired. We can order pizza and talk there," Ryan said.

We left the hospital and headed for my house. When we got to my house I went straight for the couch and laid down.

"Babe, do you want to go lay down in your bed?" Brandon asked.

"No."

"Are you sure? I will lay down with you."

"Yes." I just wanted to be around people right then.

"Okay." Brandon brushed some hair out of my face and leaned down and kissed my forehead.

I lifted my head and he sat on the couch so I could rest my head on his lap. Everyone was talking around me, but I couldn't focus on what they were saying. I tried to close my eyes but all I saw were flashes of the knife being rammed in my direction.

Instead, I laid there staring at the TV that wasn't on while everyone continued to talk around me. I wasn't paying

269

attention to what they were saying, but I heard Ryan order a few pizzas. My stomach growled and I realized I hadn't eaten since lunch over eight hours ago.

The minutes seemed liked hours as I just laid there while Brandon rubbed my head as it lay in his lap. I caught bits and pieces of the conversations that everyone was having and I heard Brandon say that he was going to go to the hospital first thing in the morning and talk to Christy.

When the pizza arrived, Brandon asked me if I wanted to eat. I was hungry but I could barely eat. After I managed to eat a slice and drink some of the diet root beer soda, I told everyone that I was going to bed.

I heard Brandon say goodnight to everyone else and he followed me to my room. I didn't realize how exhausted I was until I tried to remove my sweatshirt but could barely lift my arms. Brandon helped me change into my pajamas and then we both crawled into my bed.

I looked at the clock and it was only 10:34 p.m. What a way to spend a Friday night. We should have been out celebrating the new Seattle gym instead of lying in bed. I guess I could have been laying in a hospital bed like Christy, or worse, the morgue.

⌒ꞓ

Even though I was extremely exhausted I couldn't get the image of Christy coming after me with a knife out of my head. I tossed and turned all night. I know I kept Brandon up most of the night as well because he would hug me tighter when I turned my back towards him.

Brandon's phone alarm went off at 6:45 a.m. I think I had just fallen asleep and woke still feeling exhausted, but I knew that Brandon really wanted to get answers from Christy and I wanted to go with him to the hospital.

We arrived at the hospital a little before eight o'clock. Brandon asked the Nurse's Station what room Christy was in and when we finally found Christy's room, we saw a nurse exit and close the door behind her. Brandon slowly opened the door as he clenched my right hand. We walked into the room; the bed curtain was around the first bed. Brandon peeked in then turned to me and shook his head indicating that it wasn't Christy.

We walked a little towards the second bed that didn't have a bed curtain around it. I saw Christy laying there with her eyes closed; she looked peaceful. I noticed her medical chart was lying on a rolling table at the end of her bed. I grabbed it and scanned it quickly trying to hurry before the nurse returned.

Sure enough, Christy wasn't pregnant. The medical chart indicated that when she was admitted to the Emergency Room, they were told she was pregnant by the paramedics based on what I had told them at Brandon's condo. They did an exploratory laparoscopy... whatever that meant, and checked for the fetal heart rate, only to find that there wasn't one.

During the operation they checked for the dead fetus but found nothing. There was a note on the file saying all medical evidence concluded that she had never been pregnant. The stress and pain that she caused us over the last few months was for nothing. I slammed the chart down on the table with frustration. Brandon jumped at the noise and looked over at me.

"Sorry," I whispered. "The chart says she was never pregnant."

Before I could say anything else, Christy moved. Her eyes opened and when she saw us standing there, she started to scream. Brandon reached down and covered her mouth––I just stood there in shock.

"We're not here to hurt you, Christy. I just want some answers from you – some *honest* answers," Brandon said. "When I remove my hand, do you promise not to scream?"

Christy slowly nodded her head and looked over at me. I stood there glaring at her. Brandon removed his hand from her mouth. She didn't scream.

"We won't be long. I just want to know why you faked the pregnancy," Brandon snapped.

"I...I thought I could get you back," she whispered with a hoarse voice.

"But you were never pregnant. Didn't you think I would have noticed?"

"I was... I was going to pretend to have a miscarriage once we got back together."

"We were never going to get back together."

"I finally realized that." Christy's head drooped dejectedly.

"And that is why you tried to kill Spencer?"

She paused and swallowed hard before answering. "Yes."

"You are really fucked up in the head, you know that?" Christy didn't respond to Brandon. Instead she started to cry. "We will see you at your trial, Christy," Brandon said as he started to turn to walk out the door.

I tugged on his hand to stop him and then turned back to Christy. "I just have one question. How did you get the ultrasound?"

She didn't respond at first. Then finally she spoke, "My friend works for the doctor's office. She printed someone else's ultrasound and gave it to me."

Brandon snorted in disgust, then tugged on my hand and we left the room not saying another word to her.

⁓

We drove straight to Brandon's condo. He had received a call that it was okay for him to return home and the cops no longer needed to do anymore investigating at the condo; they had everything they needed.

We arrived at his building and took the short elevator ride up to Brandon's floor. My hands became sweaty as he held my right hand firmly. When we stepped off the elevator and walked down to Brandon's front door, we saw that his door was covered in yellow police tape.

Brandon removed the tape and unlocked his door. We both paused. "Are you sure you want to see this?" Brandon asked.

"No, but we are here. We need to clean it up and move on."

"Baby, you don't have to be strong all the time. I can clean it up."

"I know. It's okay, I can handle it."

We walked into his condo. Blood was smeared on the floor where Christy's body laid after she fell down the stairs. Black dust was dusted over the railing of the staircase. It reminded me of the TV show *Law and Order* and how the cops would dust for prints.

For the next hour we tried to get all the blood off the floor. But no matter how hard and long we scrubbed, we couldn't get it all. I had never had to clean up a pool of blood before, and apparently soap and water wouldn't work one hundred percent. Maybe it was because I knew what was there and it caught my eye more.

After we scrubbed and scrubbed, trying to erase the horrific event, we realized we weren't going to be able to get it all out on our own. Brandon stood, took my hand for me to stand and walked us over to the couch and sat down.

Brandon turned to me and started to speak, "I'm going to call someone and have them come and clean it tomorrow."

"Okay."

"The hour that we have been here has been killing me inside. All I can picture is the story you told me about what Christy did and then seeing her body laying at the bottom of the stairs."

"Me, too," I whispered.

It was hard for me to be in there, but I couldn't let Brandon deal with it all on his own. We had been a couple for only a short time, but the bonds we shared made us a team. I knew that we would overcome anything after we managed to get past this hurdle.

I loved him so much and I knew that he loved me, too. No one was going to break us apart. I managed to cheat death and we were still together, and I hoped we'd be together forever.

"I... I want to sell this condo and move," Brandon said.

"Okay, I completely understand."

"I want *us* to buy a place together. Move in with me?"

ACKNOWLEDGMENTS

First I would like to thank my husband, AG, JS, MS, SA and BP for all the advice and thoughts you have given me throughout this process. I really couldn't have done it without you all. Thank you, KA for getting me in touch with one sexy man who will
forever be on the B&S Series!

Thank you also to Teresa Mummert, Molly McAdams, Emily Snow, and R.L. Mathewson for all the advice you have given me these last few months on how to make my dream come true. I swear I owe you all one hundred margaritas each for all the questions you had to answer for me.

Also thank you to my Smutty Book Whore Mafia, Christa Cervone, Aimee P., Kim P., Nichele F. and AC Marchman – *'pimpin' ain't easy'* but you all managed to pimp out me and my book!

To Hope Welsh and Melissa S., thank you so much for all the hours you spent to review and edit my book to make **Where I Need to Be** as amazing as it could be.

And last but not least, I want to thank Joe Marvullo for giving me the hottest book cover ever...well until **Wanted** at least.

Cover Models:

Joseph Marvullo

Website: www.modelmayhem.com/jmarvullo

Facebook: www.facebook.com/ModelJosephMarvullo

Kari Jo Goodwin

Email: kari_jo14@yahoo.com

Facebook: www.facebook.com/karijomodel

Cover Photographer:

Website: www.davidmassaphoto.com

Facebook:www.facebook.com/DavidMassaPhoto

ABOUT THE AUTHOR

Kimberly Knight lives in the Bay Area in California with her loving husband and spoiled cat, Precious. In her spare time, she enjoys watching her favorite reality TV shows, playing co-ed slow pitch softball in a few local leagues, and playing computer games like World of Warcraft and online poker. However, the bulk of her time is dedicated to writing and reading Romance and Erotic fiction.

https://www.facebook.com/AuthorKKnight
https://www.facebook.com/AuthorKKnight
http://www.facebook.com/authorkimberlyknight
https://twitter.com/Author_KKnight
http://authorkknight.blogspot.com